She turned to go but then she hesitated, turning back.

'Jack, thank you for reassuring me about my name-change,' she said softly. 'It means everything to me. And thank you also for entrusting Harry to my care. I will help. I promise.'

'I know you will.'

Where had that come from? But he knew it was true. From total distrust, he now had faith.

Why? Because she told a good story? Because he'd known her as a student? Because she was forcing him to face something he'd been actively avoiding?

Or maybe it was none of those things. Maybe it was because she was standing in the moonlight in her faded jeans and her bare feet.

Maybe it was the freckles.

Maybe it was the smile. She was smiling now, quizzically, waiting for him to say goodnight and give her leave to go.

'Won't you have another drink?' he found himself saying.

She looked at him then—really looked—and he was reminded of the looks she'd given him when he was fooling round in the lab at med school, when time was starting to run out, when she was reminding him that they were there to work. And he remembered suddenly how much he'd wanted to ask her out, and how frustrated he'd been when she'd knocked back his advances.

But she wasn't thinking about the past. This was all about now. This was all about Harry.

Dear Reader

Right now my family is in the midst of restoring a fisherman's cottage that's protected by so many heritage restrictions it makes my eyes water. But when bureaucracy gets the better of me I head to our local ferry, which takes me over the treacherous Rip to the entrance to Port Phillip Bay and Melbourne beyond. Why? Well, my favourite cake shop is on the other side of the Rip—though the trip does make for expensive cake! But as well as cake I get to see dolphins. If I'm lucky they'll surf in the ferry's wake, leaping in and out of the water, joyously celebrating the fact that they can beat the boat twice over. They're smart, they're funny, and I defy anyone to watch them and not forget red tape and rotting roofing iron.

So it was with interest that I read of a dolphin sanctuary in the US where traumatised kids are offered time out, swimming with these gorgeous creatures as a type of therapy. So *what if...?* I thought as I watched the dolphins surfing alongside the boat. *What if...?* are my two favourite words. They send me off on another book almost as soon as I think them. *What if* my heroine finds a way to reach wounded kids with the same dolphins that make me smile? But *what if* she's hiding secrets? *What if* she's wounded too?

My hero is truly heroic—isn't he always? But in A SECRET SHARED... Jack needs all the help he can get to win his lady and to share the secrets that guard her heart.

The dolphins are just the guys to help him!

Marion

A SECRET SHARED...

BY
MARION LENNOX

First published in Great Britain 2014
by Mills & Boon, an imprint of Harlequin (UK) Limited,
Eton House, 18-24 Paradise Road, Richmond, Surrey, TW9 1SR

© 2014 Marion Lennox

ISBN: 978-0-263-24390-1

Marion Lennox was a country kid, a tomboy and a maths nerd, but whenever she went missing her family guessed she'd be a up gum tree reading romance novels. Climbing trees and dreaming of romance—what's not to love? But it wasn't until she was on maternity leave from her 'sensible' career, teaching statistics to undergraduates, that she finally tried to write one.

Marion's now had over one hundred romances accepted for publication. She's given up climbing trees—they got too high! She dreams her stories while she walks her dog or paddles her kayak or pokes around rock pools at low tide. It's a tough life, but she's more than ready for the challenge.

Recent titles by Marion Lennox:

Mills & Boon® Medical Romance™

WAVES OF TEMPTATION
GOLD COAST ANGELS: A DOCTOR'S REDEMPTION*
MIRACLE ON KAIMOTU ISLAND†
THE SURGEON'S DOORSTEP BABY
SYDNEY HARBOUR HOSPITAL: LILY'S SCANDAL**
DYNAMITE DOC OR CHRISTMAS DAD?
THE DOCTOR AND THE RUNAWAY HEIRESS

Gold Coast Angels
**Sydney Harbour Hospital*
†Earthquake!*

Mills & Boon® Cherish™

CHRISTMAS AT THE CASTLE
SPARKS FLY WITH THE BILLIONAIRE
A BRIDE FOR THE MAVERICK MILLIONAIRE*
HER OUTBACK RESCUER*
NIKKI AND THE LONE WOLF**
MARDIE AND THE CITY SURGEON**

Journey through the Outback duet
***Banksia Bay* miniseries

Dedication

To Ray and Deb, with thanks for making our dream a reality.

Praise for
Marion Lennox:

'Marion Lennox's RESCUE AT CRADLE LAKE
is simply magical, eliciting laughter and tears
in equal measure. A keeper.'
—*RT Book Reviews*

'Best of 2010: a very rewarding read. The characters are
believable, the setting is real, and the writing is terrific.'
—*Dear Author* on
CHRISTMAS WITH HER BOSS

CHAPTER ONE

'You want to save your kid with mantra-chanting and dolphins that eat *our* fish, go ahead and waste your money. Dolphin Sanctuary plays you for a sucker, and you're walking right in.'

This was exactly what Dr Jack Kincaid didn't want to hear. He glanced at the white-faced child in his passenger seat and hoped Harry wasn't listening.

The little boy's face was blank and unresponsive, but then, it always was. Harry had hardly spoken since the car crash that had killed his parents.

'The sanctuary seems to be building a good reputation,' he said, which was all he could think of to say. He didn't want to be here but he needed petrol. The pump attendant, fat, grubby and obviously bored, had wandered out to have a word.

It was no wonder he looked bored. There'd be few cars along this road. Jack was three hundred miles from Perth, heading for one of the most remote parts of Australia. Dolphin Bay.

Dolphins. Healing. He thought of the hundreds of schmaltzy, New Age healing-type posters he'd seen in his lifetime and he felt ill.

What *was* he doing here?

'So your kid's crook?' the attendant asked, and Jack

flicked the remote. The car windows slid up soundlessly, ensuring Harry couldn't hear.

Harry didn't react. He didn't seem to notice he was being cut out of the conversation. He never seemed to notice.

'He was injured in a road accident a while back,' he said. The pump was snail slow and this guy was intent on an inquisition. He might as well accept it.

'You're his dad?'

'His uncle. His parents were killed.'

'Poor little tacker,' the man said. 'But why bring him to Dolphin Bay? What's the point? You're being conned, mate. Fishing used to be good round here, but not any more. New Age hippies have even got permission to feed them, encouraging them in from the wild.'

'How long have they been using them for healing?'

'Since that Doc Kate came. Before that it was just dolphin saving. The place's full of animal do-gooders and weirdos who think meditation's more useful than facing life straight on. If you want to know what I think, the only good dolphin's a dead dolphin. If they'd only let us shoot...'

But, praise be, the fuel tank was full. Jack produced his wallet with relief. 'Keep the change.' He wanted to be out of here, fast. 'Use it for fish bait.'

'Thanks, mate,' the man said. 'But if I were you I'd book into the motel and take the kid fishing. Much better than messing with hippies.'

That was so much what Jack was thinking that he had to agree. 'I'd go fishing in a heartbeat,' he admitted. 'But I don't have a choice.'

'You look like a man who knows his own mind. What's stopping you?'

'Women,' Jack said, before he could help himself. 'Isn't that what stops us all?'

* * *

Four-year-old Toby Linkler's death was sudden, heart-breaking—and a deep and abiding blessing.

One minute Kate was watching as Toby's mother, Amy, stood in the shallows, holding her little son close. Together they'd watched Hobble, the youngest of the trained dolphins, swim around them in circles. The little boy's face, gaunt from illness, racked from months of chemotherapy, was lit from within. He'd even chuckled.

And then, as Hobble ducked underneath and almost propelled Toby out of the water with a nudge under his backside, Toby's gaze suddenly turned inward.

Kate was four feet away and she moved fast, but by the time she reached him, the little boy was gone.

Toby's mother sobbed with shock and horror, but she didn't move. The dolphin's circles grew wider, as if standing guard. How much did the creature know? Kate wondered. This moment couldn't be intruded on and it wasn't, even by the dolphins.

'He's…he's gone,' Amy sobbed at last. 'Oh, Toby. The doctors said… They said he might…'

They had. More than one doctor had predicted seizures with the possibility of sudden death. Kate had studied Toby's notes as thoroughly as she read every patient's history. Four years old. Brain tumour. Incomplete excision twelve months ago. Chemotherapy had shown some shrinkage but eventually the growth had outstripped treatment. The last note on the history said: 'If tumour maintains its present growth rate, prognosis is weeks, not months. We suggest palliative care as required. Referral back to family doctor.'

But Amy hadn't taken Toby back to her family doctor. One of the other mums in the city hospital kids' cancer ward had told her about Dolphin Bay Sanctuary's therapy programme. Kate had had to squeeze to get them in.

Thank heaven she had, she thought now, and her thoughts were indeed a prayer. Toby had spent most of the last few days ensconced in a tiny wetsuit, floating with the dolphins that had entranced him. Kate had four dolphins she'd trusted with this frail little boy and in the end all four had been allowed to play with him. They *had* played too, making him laugh, nudging his failing little body as he'd floated on water-wings, tossing balls high in the air so they'd landed near him, retrieving them themselves if he hadn't been able to.

He'd still needed painkillers, of course, and anti-seizure medication and drugs to try and stop the massive build-up of calcium leeching from the growing tumour, but for six glorious days he'd been a little boy again. He'd experienced fun and laughter, things that had had nothing to do with the illness and surgery he'd endured and endured and endured. At night he'd slept curled up with Maisie, Kate's therapy dog. With his mum by his side, he'd seemed almost joyous.

Today he'd woken quieter, pale, and his breathing had been shallow. Kate had known time was running out. In a normal hospital she might have ordered blood tests, checked the cancer wasn't sending his calcium levels through the roof, maybe even sent him for another MRI to check how large the tumour had grown, but given his history there was little point. Toby's mother had made her choice and, weak as he'd been, Toby had been clear on the one thing he'd wanted.

'I want to swim with Hobble.'

He had, and as his mother had cradled him Toby had felt the rush of the dolphin's sleek, shining skin as he'd circled.

'He's my friend,' he'd whispered.

And now he was gone.

There was nothing to be done. There was no call for

heroics here, no desperate attempt at resuscitation. There was just the searing agony of a mother losing her child.

It was gut-wrenching. Unbearable. A void never to be filled.

But: 'I'm so glad,' Amy managed to whisper, as her racking sobs finally eased, as Kate stood waist deep in the water and gave her all the time she needed, and as Toby's body settled deeper into death. 'I'm so glad I brought him here. Oh, Kate, thank you.'

'Don't thank me,' Kate said, hugging her close and drawing her gently out of the water. 'Thank my dolphins.'

'Dr Kate's running late.' The pleasant-faced woman in Reception was welcoming, but apologetic. 'I'm sorry, Harry,' she said, and Jack felt a jolt of surprise. The woman was addressing his nephew instead of him. 'This is Maisie,' she told Harry, gesturing to a great bear of a golden-haired retriever snoozing under her desk. 'Maisie, this is Harry.' She prodded Maisie with her toe and Maisie looked up in polite enquiry. *Me? You mean me?*

'Maisie,' the receptionist said sternly, as one might chide a recalcitrant employee. 'Say hello to Harry.'

The dog rolled onto her back, stretched, sighed, then lumbered up, strode across the room, sat in front of Harry—and raised a paw.

Harry stared. The dog sat patiently, paw outstretched, until finally, tentatively, Harry took it. Jack noticed, with quiet surprise, that his nephew almost managed a smile. It wasn't quite, but it was close.

'Dr Kate is in the water, doing therapy,' the receptionist told Jack as dog and boy shook hand and paw for the second time. 'She should be finishing now. Would you like to pop down to the beach? Please don't disturb them but if you stay beyond the high-water mark you're welcome to watch.'

Jack would very much like to watch. Despite Harry's instant relaxation—he was now solemnly shaking the big dog's paw for the third time—Jack's guard was still sky high.

Why was he here? His home was in Sydney. Harry's home was in Sydney. What Harry needed was continued therapy for healing leg fractures and a decent child psychiatrist who'd finally crack his wall of traumatised silence.

But he'd found Harry some very good child psychiatrists, and none of them had made a dent in his misery. This was desperation. It had been his Aunt Helen's idea, not his, but she had been prepared to relinquish Harry into Jack's care if he agreed to bring him.

Was it worth the risk?

'Would you like to go to the beach or stay here with Maisie?' the receptionist was asking Harry, and Harry looked at Maisie and nodded. This was a miracle all on its own. He'd been limp since the car crash, simply doing what the adults around him ordered. Three months ago he'd been a normal seven-year-old, maybe a little cosseted, maybe a little intense, but secure and loved and happy. Now, without his parents, he was simply...lost.

'You're sure?' Jack asked, and of course there was no response. But Harry was kneeling on the floor with the dog and the dog was edging sideways. Jack could see what she was doing. There was a ball, three feet away, and Maisie was looking at it with more than a canine hint.

Jack nudged it close and Maisie grabbed it and dropped it at Harry's feet. Then she backed two feet away, crouching, quivering and staring straight at Harry with all the concentration a golden retriever could summon.

Harry stared at Maisie. Maisie stared at Harry. The whole room held its breath.

And then Harry very tentatively picked up the well-chewed ball—and tossed it about four feet.

Maisie pounced with dramatic flourish, reaching it before it hit the floor, but she wasn't content with a simple retrieval. She whirled three times, tossed the ball upwards herself and caught it again—and then came back and dropped it at Harry's feet again.

And, unbelievably, Harry giggled.

'I'll buy the dog,' Jack muttered, and the receptionist grinned.

'She's not for sale. Kate values her above diamonds. Go and watch her if you like. Harry and Maisie are safe with me.'

They were. Jack watched the little boy a moment longer and felt himself relax, which was something he didn't think he'd done once, not since his brother had died. The dog was taking care of Harry and the relief was immeasurable.

'Go,' the receptionist said gently, and her message was unmistakeable. *It's better if you're not here. Let these two bond.*

She was right. Harry didn't need him; since the accident he hadn't seemed to need anyone.

If one dog could make a difference...

He'd tried a puppy; he'd tried almost everything. But now... Whatever this crazy dolphin-mantra place was, this dog was breaking through.

Dr Jack Kincaid didn't need to be told again.

He went.

It was time to leave the water; time for the reality of death to hit home. As wonderful as this place was, it was simply time out. Toby was dead. His mother now had to start facing a world without him.

Kate's arm was around Amy's waist as they made their

way from the shallows. The world was waiting. Official-
dom would move in and there was nothing Kate could
do to protect Amy from it.

But at least she'd had this time. At least the week before Toby's death hadn't been filled with hospitals, drips,
rush. Her dolphins had helped.

She turned for a moment as she reached the beach;
they both did. Far out in the deep water, Hobble still
seemed to be watching them. He was doing sweeping
curves at the outer limits of the pool. At the far reaches
of each curve he leaped from the water towards them,
and then dived deep, again and again.

'Thank you,' Amy whispered toward him, and who
knew if the dolphin could understand. But no matter what
their level of understanding, the dolphins had helped ease
one little boy's passing.

Kate had more patients waiting. She needed to move
on, but what had just happened had eased the pain around
her own heart a little as well.

Jack walked over the ridge of sandbank just as the two
women turned to walk up the beach. Two women and
a child. The women were dressed in plain blue stinger
suits. The child was in a wetsuit.

The child was dead.

Jack Kincaid had been a doctor long enough to sense
it even as he saw it. The child was cradled in the shorter
woman's arms, the woman was sobbing, and every step
they took spelled defeat.

What the…?

He broke into a run. If the child had gone underwater,
it might not be too late. Why wasn't anyone doing CPR?
Had they tried and failed? In children there was sometimes success when all hope was lost. He had his phone

out, hitting the emergency quick-dial, thinking paramed-ics, oxygen, help…

'Don't phone.' The taller woman's voice was a curt command, urgent enough to make him pause. The other woman was sinking to her knees, still cradling the child. 'What the hell…?'

'It's okay.'

What sort of crazy was this? He reached them and he would have knelt by the child but the woman held him back.

'I'm Dr Kate,' she said. 'I'm so sorry you had to see this but, believe me, it's okay.'

'How can it be okay?'

'Toby's had cancer,' she said, softly so as not to break into the other woman's grief. She took his arm, draw-ing him away a little, giving woman and child space. 'He's had brain metastases. He was terminally ill. This afternoon he's been playing with the dolphins, he had a seizure and he died. There was nothing we could do.'

'Did you try?' Jack demanded, incredulous. A sei-zure… He thought of all the things that could be done in a major city hospital, the drugs that could stop a seizure, the resuscitation equipment. 'Surely…'

'Amy wanted it this way,' Kate said. 'She has the right to make a choice on behalf of her son and I think it was a good one.' She hesitated and then glanced at her watch. 'You'll be Harry's guardian,' she said. 'I'm sorry I'm run-ning late but you understand…' She gestured to woman and child. 'Some things have to take precedence. Has Maisie settled your Harry?'

Maisie…the dog. She was depending on her dog to settle a new patient?

But, then, Maisie *had* settled Harry, better than ever he could have.

'Yes,' he conceded, dragging his eyes away from the distraught mother and child.

'I'm glad,' she said, and she smiled.

And in that moment time stood still. What the…?

He knew this woman! He knew her very well indeed. Dr Catherine Heineman. They'd been students together. Tutorial partners. Friends.

He hadn't seen her since…since…

'You're…Doctor Kate?' His tone was incredulous.

'I'm Kate Martin,' the woman said simply. 'Dr Kate Martin.'

'You're Cathy.'

Her face lost its colour. She stared up at him and took an instinctive step backward.

'What nonsense is this?' He'd read the blurb for the dolphin sanctuary. The healing part of it was run by one Dr Kate Martin, this woman. According to the blurb she had qualifications in physiotherapy and counselling. Deeply suspicious, he'd checked, but the qualifications had been conferred by one of the most prestigious universities in New Zealand.

That didn't fit at all with what he was seeing here now, with what he knew. This woman was in her early thirties maybe. He'd last seen Cathy in her early twenties but it didn't stop him knowing her.

'You're Cathy,' he said again, and he saw her flinch.

'I can explain.'

She'd better. Counsellor with training in psychology? Physiotherapist? Had she abandoned her medical degree and retrained in another country? Under another name? Why? Had she been struck off the medical register?

He stared at her and saw shadows. She was five feet eight or so, and a bit too thin. At university he'd thought her attractive. Very attractive. Now she looked…gaunt? Her chestnut hair was tugged into a practical knot. Her blue all-in-one stinger suit was deeply unflattering. Her green eyes, which had flashed with laughter when he'd messed up a lab trial or someone had made a joke, didn't look like they did much laughing now.

Unregistered? Hiding? Why?

Drugs? Drug-taking was the most common reason for doctors being deregistered and instinctively his gaze fell to her arms, looking for track marks. The sleeves of her stinger suit were pulled up. Her forearms were clean, but she saw where his gaze went and stepped back as if he'd struck her.

'It's not what you think. I can explain.'

'You'd better.' If he'd dragged Harry all the way across the country to have him treated by an unregistered doctor...

'I can't now.' She closed her eyes for a millisecond, that was all, but when she opened them she seemed to have recovered. The look she gave him was direct and firm. 'I need to stay with Amy and Toby. Yes, I'm Cathy but I'm also Kate. I'd ask that you keep that to yourself until you hear my explanation.' She ran her fingers wearily through her hair and the formal knot gave a little, letting a couple of chestnut tendrils escape. It made her look younger, and somehow more vulnerable. 'Could you bring your nephew and Maisie down to the beach? Build a sandcastle. Give me some time. Please?'

And then she was gone, heading back to the woman and her child, stooping to help mother lift the lifeless body of her son. Together they carried him up the beach and away.

Jack was left staring after her.

CHAPTER TWO

HE COULDN'T BELIEVE it. Kate Martin, physiotherapist and counsellor, medical director of Dolphin Bay Healing Resort, had transformed into Cathy Heineman who'd shared his undergraduate student life.

Cathy had been his friend, and in truth he wouldn't have minded if she'd been more than that. She'd been vibrant, fun and beautiful. But she'd also been a little aloof. She hadn't talked about her private life and she'd laughed off any advances. Friendship only, she'd decreed, though sometimes he'd wondered... When they'd stayed back late, working together, he'd thought there had been this attraction. Surely it had been mutual.

But it obviously hadn't been. In fourth year she'd turned up after the summer holidays sporting a wedding ring.

'Simon and I have been planning to wed since childhood,' she'd told him, and that was pretty much all she'd said. He'd never met her husband—no one had. Neither had the student cohort seen much of Cathy after that. She'd attended lectures but the old camaraderie had gone.

She hadn't even attended graduation. 'She requested her degrees be posted to her,' he'd heard. Someone had said she'd moved to Melbourne to do her internship and that was the last he'd heard of her.

And now... His head was spinning with questions,

but overriding everything else was the knowledge that he would not expose his nephew to treatment by anyone who was dishonest.

The Cathy he'd known had been brilliant.

The Cathy he'd just seen had been helping a dead child from the water. She was in a suspect place doing suspect things, and his nephew's welfare was at stake.

Get out of here now.

His phone rang. It'd be Helen, he thought. The road here had been almost completely lacking phone reception. There was only the faintest of signals now. Helen wouldn't have been able to ring him for hours. She'd be frantic.

'Where are you?' Her tone was accusatory.

'I'm at the dolphin sanctuary, of course.'

Helen's breath exhaled in a rush. 'You made it? Is it good? Oh, Jack, will it make a difference?'

'So far I've seen a dead child and a doctor who's not who she says she is,' he said bluntly. 'Helen, do you remember Cathy Heineman? She was a med student with Don and me. She faded from the social scene after fourth year. Remember?'

'The clever one you did your lab work with,' Helen said. Helen had five children under ten. She was still mourning her brother's death, but her mind was like a steel trap. She'd done dentistry while her brother, Arthur, had done medicine with Jack. Arthur and Jack had been mates, and in turn Helen had become best friends with Jack's sister, Beth. Arthur and Beth had married, bringing them even closer. They'd all been at university together and they knew each other's friends.

So she knew Cathy. Kate.

'The whisper was that the guy she married was possessive,' she said, turning obligingly thoughtful. 'He wouldn't let her out of his sight. No one saw much of her after her wedding and not at all after we graduated.'

'She's here. She's practising as a physiotherapist and counsellor. The whole place smells fishy.'

'Well, it is a dolphin sanctuary.'

'Helen…'

'Look, you promised to give it a go,' Helen said bluntly. 'Kate, Cathy, who gives a toss what she calls herself if it has a chance of working? You know I'd be there with him myself but I'd have had to bring the babies with me.'

She would. That was what this whole disaster was about. Helen was an earth mother, parent of five noisy, exuberant children, generous to a fault. She and her amiable husband had been more than ready to take their newly orphaned nephew into their expanding brood.

It had seemed the perfect solution. Helen was Harry's aunt, she loved him to bits, she was married and stable and able to take care of him.

Jack was Harry's uncle but he was single. He was a rising star in his chosen field of oncology, he had little intention of settling down, and there was no reason that he should take on his seven-year-old nephew.

Except…

Except that one wounded little boy had been failing to thrive within Helen's noisy throng. Harry had always been quiet and a little introspective, and the loss of his parents, plus the shocking injuries to his leg, had seen him withdraw into himself.

The last time Jack had gone to see him he'd refused to come out of the bedroom he'd been sharing with one of his cousins. Helen had shown him literature on this place. 'It can't do any harm,' she'd told him. 'I'll farm the three eldest out and the babies can come with us. Doug won't mind, will you, darling?' She'd smiled fondly at her long-suffering husband. 'We do what we must for each of our children and Harry's the same.'

Only Harry wasn't the same. Jack had watched him that night, pushing his food from side to side on his plate, mentally absent from the noise and jostling about him, and he'd made a decision.

'Let me take care of him for a while. I'll take a few weeks off work. Maybe he'll be happier with me.'

Afterwards he hadn't been able to believe he'd said it. He knew nothing about children—zip. His current girl-friend, Annalise, had been appalled.'

'Well, don't expect me to help. Children and me... Darling, I'm a radiologist, not a childminder.

He was an oncologist, not a childminder either, but for the last two weeks he'd been doing his best.

But not getting through.

'But you will take him to this place,' Helen had de-creed, flourishing the literature at him. 'I swear, Jack, it sounds just what he needs.'

'He needs time, not quackery.'

'If you don't take him, I will. Jack, I'll fight you for this. I should make the decisions. You're not capable of caring for him and I am.'

And there it was, out in the open. They were joint guardians. On the surface they had equal claims to guard-ianship, but Helen had the home, the experience, the love.

He should stand aside and leave her to it. Only Harry's desolation prevented it.

Taking him to the dolphin sanctuary had been a test, he thought. Helen—and others—wanted proof he was serious about this parenting role.

The problem was that he wasn't sure that he was se-rious about parenting himself, especially as he'd been sole carer for two weeks now and made not one dint in the little boy's misery.

Until this afternoon, when one bear of a dog had made Harry giggle.

'I'll find out about Cathy,' Helen offered, speaking urgently now. 'I'll make enquiries. But unless it's really awful, you should still give the place a chance.'

'I told you, Helen, I've been here half an hour and already there's a child dead.'

'There must be a reason.'

'A brain tumour,' he conceded.

'They do palliative care work as well. You'd expect—'

'I'd expect resuscitation efforts on a four-year-old.'

'Give it more than half an hour,' Helen said urgently. 'It's taken me all the contacts we have and then some to get him into the place. Believe it or not, there's a queue months long. Don't you dare walk away.'

'And if it's dangerous?'

'You stay with him all the time. Bond. This is what you wanted, Jack. Now's the time to step up to the mark.'

And he knew it was.

Kate did what she could for Amy and for her little son. Amy's mother and sister had spent the last week here as well. Other arms enfolded the distraught mother, freeing Kate to leave her in their care. In the end she backed out unnoticed, as grandmother, mother and aunt collectively said goodbye to their little boy.

She put herself on autopilot for a while, filling in forms, phoning the coroner, clearing the way for funeral directors to fly Toby and his family directly back to Queensland, where they'd lived. She headed back to her bungalow and showered. Then she stood on her veranda and stared out to sea for a while, trying to get Toby's death in perspective. Impossible, but she had to try, just like she always did. Other children needed her. Somehow she'd learned to move on.

She'd learned to move on from a lot, she conceded, and part of that was her history. And her history included Jack Kincaid.

It had been such a shock to see him.

Jack. His name echoed over and over in Kate's head and she felt ill.

She couldn't be ill. Jack's nephew was her next client. Jack Kincaid was waiting for her to finish the formalities with Toby and his mother. Jack Kincaid had to be faced.

But maybe he wouldn't wait. She'd seen his horror when he'd realised Toby was dead; when he'd seen that she wasn't fighting to prolong his life.

She might have got Toby back, she conceded. If she'd tried CPR, had had oxygen on the beach, had fought with every medical skill she had, Toby might still be alive. He'd be unconscious, though. They all knew the tumour was massive and unresponsive to any more chemotherapy or radiation. If she'd fought he could have had maybe a week, maybe even longer, on oxygen, on life support, but his mother hadn't wanted that. No one had wanted it.

She hadn't had to flinch at the condemnation in Jack Kincaid's eyes. She had not one single regret over her care of Toby.

But what would she tell him? Jack had been a friend at medical school. If he was still here she needed to give him an explanation. What?

The truth? Did she trust him enough for that?

She might have no choice. It seemed Harry was Jack's nephew, Jack's sister's child. If she'd recognised the name she would never have accepted him as a client, but the booking had been done by a woman with a name as unfamiliar as all the names she so carefully vetted. Harry had been supposed to be coming with someone called Helen.

No matter. Chinks of her old life were bound to intrude sooner or later. She'd known that. It was just...she'd hoped it would be later.

She thought back to the Jack she'd known over ten years ago. He'd been acutely intelligent, intuitive and skilled. On top of that he'd been drop-dead gorgeous. Tall with dark hair and strong bone structure, always tanned, almost too good looking for his own good, and his dark eyes had always gleamed with mischief. Maturity had only added to his looks, she conceded, but it was the Jack of years ago she was thinking of now. If there had been pranks to be played, Jack had always been at the centre. If there had been a beautiful woman to be dated, Jack had been right there, too.

Early on they were allocated as partners in the science component of their course. They suited each other as study mates. Her seriousness didn't distract him, and his intelligence and humour pleased her. But his dating habits were legend. 'You should have a harem,' she told him. 'That way you wouldn't have to date one by one. You could have them all together.'

'I'd rather that than be stuck with one person for ever from sixteen,' he retorted. She finally told him of Simon's existence when he... When they... Well, late one night things got a little out of hand and she had to tell him the truth. That she had a boyfriend. That she'd had a boyfriend for years so she couldn't be attracted to Jack.

'Monogamy for life from sixteen?' he mocked. 'You must be out of your mind.'

Later, when his words proved true—for it seemed that she had indeed been out of her mind—she'd lie awake in the small hours and think about how different life could have been if she hadn't been a good girl. How it could have been if she'd been able to forget family obligations. If she'd given in to the attraction she'd surely felt.

Move on, she told herself harshly. The time for regrets

was well and truly past. What she needed to focus on now was calming Jack down, persuading him to either let her treat his little nephew or tear up the contract and leave.

But whatever way he went, she had to gain his silence.

On impulse she headed indoors and hit the internet. Jack Kincaid.

Professor Jack Kincaid. Head of Oncology at Sydney Central. Research qualifications to make an academic's eyes water. Medical practice extraordinary. His early promise had been met and more; this man was seriously skilled, seriously qualified. More, as she flicked through the site she found links to patients' opinions of the man who'd treated them.

Seriously good. Seriously kind. Empathic. A workaholic by the look of it.

But he'd booked in here for two weeks. Two weeks of this man's time looked to be an incredible commitment.

Okay, she was impressed, but she was also scared. This wasn't a man to be deflected with weak excuses. It'd be the truth or nothing, if he decided to stay.

She headed back to work, and found herself almost hoping he'd decide to leave. That'd make her life a whole lot less complicated.

They had to wait for over an hour, and every minute brought fresh doubts.

He took Harry for a walk around the resort. There were a dozen bungalows built on the beachfront, with dolphins painted on their front doors. Wind chimes hung from their verandas and brightly coloured hammocks hung from the veranda rails.

Sand spits covered with stunted eucalypts reached out from both sides of the resort, the spits forming a secluded bay. A great sweep of netting enclosed half the cove. That'd be a pool for what the information sheet told him were the captive dolphins. These, according to his sheet, were either dolphins who'd been injured in some way or who'd been raised in some form of captivity and brought here in an attempt to rehabilitate them to the wild.

Some dolphins could never be rehabilitated, the sheet said, and these were the dolphins trained to interact with the resort's clients. Their injuries were so bad or they'd learned to be too dependent on humans to ever survive in the wild.

Jack and Harry wandered down to the beach again, hand in hand. Harry had fallen back into silence as he always did. For the last three months he'd simply done what he was told.

He still walked with a heavy limp—his left leg still needed to be braced. He stumped along and Jack's heart twisted for him.

One stupid moment of speed and carelessness. Metal on metal. Lives changed for ever.

There was a scattering of people on the beach, well away from the netted area where Toby had died. These must be more of the resort's clients, he thought, as this place was too far for tourists to come. There were gay little beach shelters scattered about for whoever wanted or needed shade. A couple of kids were in beach-tyred wheelchairs. A few kids were playing in the shallows. Parents were playing with them, talking among themselves.

He had no wish to join them. Did he have any intention of staying?

'Maisie,' Harry said, dragging his thoughts back from introspection, and he glanced back to where the little boy was looking and saw the big golden retriever bounding down the beach towards them. Carrying a ball. She raced straight up to them, dropped the ball at Harry's feet, then bounced backwards and beamed with a full-on canine beam.

'Toss it,' Jack suggested. Harry hesitated but Maisie was practically turning herself inside out with ball-need.

Finally Harry picked the ball up and threw it all of three feet.

The big dog pounced, but before bringing it back she raced towards the shore, dropped it into the shallows, quivered and then brought it back to them. Her message couldn't be clearer. *Throw it further. Throw it into the sea.*

'You throw it,' Harry whispered, and such a command was almost unheard of from Harry.

So Jack threw it, to the water's edge. The dog retrieved it with joy but this time she took it further into the shallows before bringing it back.

Once again her message was clear. 'Throw it even further.'

'She wants you to throw it deep,' Harry whispered, so Jack did. He hurled the ball out to where the waves were just breaking.

Maisie was on it like a bullet, streaking through the water, diving through the waves, reaching the ball...

But then not stopping.

The reason the waves were so shallow here, why the beach was so safe, was that the outer spits curved around, protecting the inner bay. At low tide the spits would be connected to the land but now, at high tide, the sand spits formed long, narrow islands. The island looked beautiful, sand washed and untouched, apart from a host of sandpipers searching for pippies or crabs or sand fleas— whatever sandpipers ate.

And now Maisie was headed for the spit island as well. She swam strongly until she reached it, then raced onto the sand, sending sandpipers scattering in alarm.

But then she turned and looked back at the beach. She looked at the water between herself and the shore.

She looked at Jack and Harry. She dropped her ball at her feet—and she shivered.

She was maybe fifty yards from them, through breast-deep water. She'd swum out with ease but her demeanour now was unmistakeable. *How have I got here? Uh-oh.*

'She's stuck,' Harry gasped, appalled.

'She can swim back.'

'She's scared.'

She couldn't be. Jack stared at the dog in exasperation. She'd swum through the shallow waves with ease. Of course she could get back.

He glanced along the beach, hoping someone official might appear, but it must be time to pack up. The few people left on the beach were two or three hundred yards away, gathering belongings, packing up the beach shelters, heading up through the sand tracks to the resort.

What was he supposed to do? Stand and yell, 'Help, the dog is stuck, save her'?

'Maisie,' he yelled, in what he hoped was his most authoritative voice. 'Come.'

The big dog quivered some more—and then as the last of the beachgoers disappeared over the sand dunes, she started to howl.

'Help her,' Harry said in horror. 'Jack, help her.'

And there was another first. Not once in three months had Harry called Jack by name. Not once had he asked for anything.

Jack, help her.

'She can swim back herself.'

'She's frightened,' Harry whispered. 'What if a big wave comes and washes her off?'

'Then she'll have to swim.'

'But she's scared.' And as if confirmation was necessary, Maisie's howls grew louder. She squatted on the sand and shivered, every inch of her proclaiming she was one terrified mutt, stranded on a desert island for ever, doomed to starve to death or drown on an incoming tide.

'Jack…' Harry whispered. 'Jack!'

And a man had to do what a man had to do.

'If I swim out and fetch her, promise you won't move from here,' Jack told his nephew, and Harry nodded.

'Hurry.'

Maisie was now crouching low, as if the sand was about to give way beneath her. Her howls had given way to whimpers. Loud whimpers.

'Promise out loud,' Jack demanded of Harry.

'I promise.'

The kid had talked. Even if he took him home now, the barrier of silence had been broken. Great, he thought grimly. Now all I have to do is rescue one stupid dog.

He hauled off his shoes, shirt and pants, thanking fate that he was wearing decent boxers. He hesitated for a moment, thinking he really didn't want to leave Harry on the beach, but Harry met his gaze head on.

'I promise,' he said again, and it was enough. The two words were a joy all by themselves. They were almost enough to make him turn to the water with enthusiasm, to plough into the shallows, to dive through the waves, to swim the twenty or so strokes it took him to reach the island spit.

Finally he hauled himself out of the water and headed for Maisie…who waited until he was less than six feet from her and then bounded to her feet, grabbed her ball, launched herself back into the water and headed for shore.

Jack was left standing on his island in his boxers, staring helplessly after her.

Maisie made it back with no effort at all. She bounded

up the beach to Harry, dropped the ball at his feet and turned to stare out at Jack.

Her tail was whirring like a helicopter. Even from where he was Jack could sense the grin. This was a great dog con.

She walked over the sand hill and saw Jack in the water. She could see at a glance what had happened. Maisie the jokester dog. This trick almost always worked. Occasionally a parent reacted with anger but usually it was laughter, and Kate could see Jack's laughter from where she stood. He watched the dog paddle effortlessly through the shallows to the beach and she saw his shoulders shake.

She was smiling as well. So the humour remained.

She'd liked this man.

She'd also thought he was gorgeous—and he still was. He'd stripped to his boxers. He stood in the sunlight, the late afternoon rays glinting on his wet body. Even from here she could see the power of the man. He must work out at some time in his seriously impressive schedule, she thought. He looked ripped.

She watched as he headed back into the water, diving into the shallows, diving under, taking a few long, strong strokes before he caught a wave that took him all the way to shore.

Harry and Maisie were waiting, Maisie tail-wagging as if she'd pulled off the world's best joke, Harry looking worried.

Jack strode out of the water, lifted his small nephew and swung him in a big, wet circle.

'She fooled us,' he told Harry. 'Don't look so worried. The doggy fooled us both. Isn't she clever?'

Harry gave a tight little smile. His rigid body didn't unbend, however, and after a moment Jack put him down.

'This is a very strange place,' he told Harry. 'Do you

know, I think it might even be fun. I'm not sure yet, but maybe we should give it a try.'

To be fooled by a dog was one thing. To be fooled by a woman you didn't trust was another. He set Harry down, looked up, and Cathy was there. Or Kate. Whichever, both of them were laughing.

'I'm sorry. Donna should have warned you. Maisie always tries that on.'

'Donna?' he said dangerously.

'Our receptionist. She's supposed to warn everyone. This is Maisie's favourite party trick to get adults into the water. Strangely, she never tries it on kids. Only adults. She's so clever.'

'Right,' Jack growled. To say he was feeling at a disadvantage was an understatement. He was dripping. He was in his boxers. On the other hand, Kate had obviously cleaned up after her time with Toby. She was wearing a soft blue skirt and white blouse. Her hair was neatly curled on top of her head. She looked fresh, professional...and deeply amused, but...

'Maisie saved herself,' Harry pronounced, and he was talking again. That was almost enough to make Jack forget about Kate. Almost. Her chuckle had him entranced.

Kate wasn't his type. She'd never really been his type, he conceded. Yes, there had been that initial attraction but he liked his women cool, sophisticated.

Kate was cute rather than classically beautiful, he thought. She had freckles. Lots of freckles.

She looked like the girl next door, he thought. So why was he looking at a pair of laughing eyes and thinking... thinking...

He didn't need to think in that direction. She'd always had secrets and he didn't like it. This woman had some hidden agenda and Harry's welfare was at stake. He needed to find out what was going on.

But Kate was no longer looking at him. She'd stooped to crouch before Harry.

'Hi,' she said. 'I'm Kate, Maisie's mother. I hear your uncle has brought you here to stay for a few days so you can meet Maisie and my friends, the dolphins.'

Harry was back to saying nothing. Kate, however, didn't appear in the least bit disconcerted. She rose, headed over the sandhill and came back carrying a bucket. Of fish.

'I dumped these when I saw your uncle saving Maisie,' she said, returning to them. 'Wasn't he brave? But isn't Maisie clever to trick him? Jack, would you like to go and get dry while Harry and I feed the dolphins? Would you like a little time out?'

It was exactly what he'd like. He was feeling...exposed. He was bare chested, bare legged and a bit chilly now the sun was sinking low, but he still had reservations about this woman. He wasn't about to leave her alone with his nephew until he knew more.

Harry was still not speaking, but he was peering into the bucket. Fish!

'These are a snack for the wild dolphins,' Kate said, talking exclusively to Harry. 'We feed the dolphins in the healing pool, but every now and then we give our wild dolphins a treat. Some of the wild dolphins are ones we've treated here for injuries and let go, but most are just free dolphins who come to say hello. If we encourage them to stick around, when we have an injured dolphin who's better we can release him into a group of friends. Do you think that's a good idea?'

Harry nodded.

Jack had resolved not to trust this woman, but every ounce of Kate's attention was focussed on Harry. He thought, It doesn't matter if I trust or not, but if Harry trusts…

He had to stick with him. He wasn't going as far as letting this woman take over but something seemed to be working. He hauled his shirt over his still-damp torso and took Harry's hand.

Harry didn't respond. There was never a moment when those small fingers curled around his. He trusted no one.

'Where do you feed them?' he asked, and she motioned to where the net divided the free bay from the pool.

'At the boundary. I feed those in the pool and out so they see each other.'

'But the pool ones can't get out?' Harry asked, and once more Jack held his breath.

'The ones in the pool all have something wrong with them,' Kate said, starting to walk down to the water, leaving them to follow if they willed. And, of course, they willed. Harry was moving even before Jack led. 'If we let them out into the ocean they'll die. But we've made the pool enormous and we try and make them feel as free as we can.'

They reached the netted boundary. She walked into the water—she might look professional from the knees up but she had bare feet—and she lifted a fish out of the bucket. She slapped the surface a few times with the fish and she yelled.

'Grub's up. Come and get it.'

He was as fascinated as Harry. They stood on the shoreline and watched as far out a fin appeared and then another and another. And then there was a line of eight dolphins, surfing in on a wave to reach the shallows. They paused as a group in about two feet of water, and a couple reared back as if standing on tiptoe, watching.

And in the enclosure four more dolphins assembled and did the same, so Kate had a dozen dolphins at attention.

'Now, the trick is, one fish each,' she told Harry. 'And they're very tricky. Every time one gets a fish he pretends that he hasn't. So the ones who do the most jumping up and down and pleading are the ones who've had a fish. The others know I'm fair and if they wait their turn they'll get one.'

She lifted the fish—a fish Jack thought was a good breakfast size—and tossed it to the first wild dolphin. He caught it with dexterity. She then tossed a fish to each wild dolphin in turn. She was right, the ones who'd been fed became sneaky but Kate was sneakier still, and not one dolphin got more than his share.

'If we feed them too much they won't bother to hunt themselves,' she told Harry briskly, as she moved from the outer rim of the pool to the inner. 'And that'd never do. Now, would you like to give one of my tame guys a fish?'

Without waiting for an answer, she delved in the bucket, snagged a fish and held it up. 'This would make a good meal for me. Our dolphins get very well fed. Harry, if you'd like to meet my friends, the closest is Hobble. The next one is Bubbles. Then we have Smiley and Squirt. If you and your uncle decide to stay here for a while then you'll meet them close up. They like playing with a ball just as much as Maisie does.'

But it was enough. Harry closed up, as he'd closed up for months. Jack felt him withdraw, felt his small body clench with tension, felt his hand become rigid in his clasp.

Did Kate know how much progress he'd made in the last hour? he wondered.

'Maybe we need to stop...' he started, but Kate was there before him.

'Only if you want, of course,' she said cheerfully. 'You decide, but if you stay you'll have a nice little bedroom overlooking the sea. Some people who come here stay in bed the whole time and every now and then they peek through the curtains at the dolphins. That's all they want to do and it's why we call it a sanctuary. Everyone here is allowed to do exactly what they want to do. Now, I gather Donna has shown you your bungalow? It's the yellow one, and your bedroom is all yellow, too. If you want you can go there now. Dinner's in the dining room in half an hour but if you want to you can have it in your little house. There's a menu on the wall. We have everything from sausage rolls to pizza to great big hamburgers for your uncle. But you decide. Harry, I'm going to feed the rest of my dolphins now, but you can do whatever you want.'

It was exactly the right thing to say. Harry didn't move. The tension was still there but he'd been given an escape route. The pressure was off and if he wanted he could still stay and watch.

He didn't say a word but neither did he pull back, retreat, head for the safety of the cute little bungalow that was to be their home for the next two weeks.

Instead, he stood silent. His hand was still in Jack's, not responsive, not clinging but not pulling away either. They watched in silence as Kate waded into the pool and spoke to her four tame dolphins. She showed each of them a fish and asked them to spin three times and do a belly roll before she handed them—formally, it seemed—their supper.

Then she backed out of the water, waved to the dolphins and waved to them with the same cheer.

'See you later,' she said. 'Have a good night. Harry, the sausage rolls are great and the pizza's better. If you see me when you're peeking through your curtains to-morrow, can you give me a wave?'

And she was gone, clicking her fingers so Maisie fell in behind her. She was a formal, professional...doctor? A doctor with bare feet, an empty fish bucket and a be-draggled, soaking dog.

What sort of place had he landed himself in?

What sort of woman had Cathy...Kate...become?

He didn't know. All he knew was that the tension had once again gone out of his little nephew.

'I need to take a shower,' he told Harry. 'I'm all wet.'

He didn't expect an answer but it came. 'The dog made you wet,' Harry said.

He grinned. 'She certainly did. Would you like pizza?'

'Yes,' said Harry, and Jack knew that whatever Cathy/Kate was, whatever she'd become, he needed to take a chance on this place.

He needed to take a chance on her.

CHAPTER THREE

HARRY RETREATED AGAIN into silence. Jack ordered via the cabin phone for them both—pizza and orange juice for Harry, a hamburger and beer for himself. A cheerful lass with a strong Canadian accent arrived at their bungalow fifteen minutes later, chatted happily to Jack and Harry, didn't seem to mind that Harry didn't respond, left their dinner and left them to the night.

They sat on their little balcony, a table between them, and watched the sun set over the ocean. They could see the dolphin pool from here. From time to time a dolphin broke the surface, the ripples spreading as if dispersing the tangerine rays of the setting sun. The gentle hush-hush of the breaking waves was all the sound there was.

No pressure, Jack thought. If Harry was at Helen's right now, the whole family would be pressuring him to eat. Even Helen's kids knew Harry didn't eat enough, so every time he took a bite was cause for family celebration.

Not here. Jack was taking a leaf out of Kate's book, backing off.

During the journey he'd insisted Harry eat, playing the heavy-handed uncle.

'I don't care if you don't want it, Harry, but you'll get sick if you don't eat. Six mouthfuls or you're not leaving the table.'

Now, at this place, it seemed less urgent. This seemed the time when they could both start again.

He ate his hamburger—extremely large, extremely good. He drank his beer and watched the sunset and didn't say a word, and as he finished his food a small hand snagged a piece of pizza. He didn't comment and when the lass came to collect the empty tray neither did she.

'Dr Kate says she might drop by later to have a chat,' she told Jack cheerfully. 'There are forms to fill in. Boring. She says there's no need to stay up if you don't want. It can wait until morning, but she'll drop by anyway.'

And Jack figured what this was about, too. Their formal appointment this afternoon had been missed. Kate would come—he'd expected it—but by forewarning them both, Harry would be reassured. If the little boy woke and heard voices he'd know what was happening. Harry needed no surprises, no shocks, no worries. He needed his world to stabilise again—if it ever could.

To lose both his parents in the one appalling moment...Jack could hardly imagine the black hole it had created. To be seven and to lose so much...

A shadow emerged from the trees, sniffing up the steps as the girl removed the tray and prepared to leave.

'Maisie,' the girl said. She smiled and turned to Harry. 'Harry, Maisie's very fussy,' she said. 'Every night she decides who she'd like to sleep with. It seems tonight she's chosen you. If you don't want her, I'll take her away with me now. She has her own bed with Dr Kate. We don't want her to be a bother.'

Harry didn't answer but it didn't trouble Maisie. The big dog proceeded ponderously up the steps and put his great head on Harry's knee. And sighed.

Her message couldn't be more clear. *No one in this world understands me. You're my only friend. Please let me stay.*

She put her paw up in silent entreaty. Harry cast a covert glance at Jack and then back at Maisie.

'C-can she stay?'

'Only if she sleeps on your bed,' Jack said sternly. 'I don't like dogs snoring on mine.'

'D-does she snore?'

'Sometimes,' the lass said cheerfully. 'Will I take her away?'

'N-no,' Harry managed, and the thing was settled. So half an hour later boy and dog were tucked up in bed. Harry's arms were firmly around Maisie's neck and Harry was fast asleep.

Helen had a dog. They'd also tried him out with a puppy but they'd got nowhere.

This dog, though, knew all the right moves. She knew just how to wriggle her way under a small boy's defences.

Like Kate was doing?

He'd walked into this place and felt deeply suspicious. What kind of a healing centre didn't try to save a child? Even if the explanation of terminal illness was true, why was no doctor in attendance? Kate was listed in the resort's advertising as being a physiotherapist and a counsellor. There was no mention of her being a medical doctor. Something must have gone horribly wrong with her career. He didn't trust her, and yet somehow he'd agreed to stay. By reaching out to Harry, she'd wriggled under his defences and he was left feeling more than a little vulnerable.

He didn't like it. Jack liked control. He had no kids himself. Now he had one small nephew who'd managed to touch his heart and leave him exposed. To charlatans? To a woman who called herself Kate but who wasn't.

'Jack?'

The voice was so soft he hardly heard it, but he'd been waiting.

Kate? Cathy.

The sun had sunk over the horizon; the merest hint of colour tinging the point where the sea disappeared towards Africa. The night was warm and still. No sound came from other bungalows. What sort of resort was this when by eight o'clock everyone seemed asleep?

'Hi,' Kate said, as she reached the steps. 'I have some forms for you to fill in, and some questions I need answered. Is now a good time?'

She was casually dressed, in jeans with a slouchy windcheater over the top. Her feet were still bare. The only hint of professionalism was the two thick envelopes she carried.

She'd let her hair out, he thought inconsequentially. It was curly and bouncy and touched her shoulders. Nice.

Um...don't go there. This is Harry's welfare, he told himself. Be professional.

'I need to throw you more questions than you throw at me,' he growled. 'What are you playing at?'

She was halfway up the veranda steps and she paused. 'You sound angry.'

'Why wouldn't I be angry? This is my sister's child. I'm responsible for him. You're not who you say you are. I don't want anyone messing with his welfare.'

'Do you think I could possibly hurt Harry?'

'I don't know what game you're playing...'

'No game,' she said stiffly. 'This place represents me exactly as I am. I'm Kate Martin, counsellor and physiotherapist.'

'You and I both know that's a lie.'

'It isn't a lie. I trained at university in Auckland. Years of study. My qualifications are real.'

'You're a doctor, or you were. Have you been struck off?'

'No,' she said flatly, defiantly. 'I haven't. But it's my choice whether I advertise my medical degree or not. With my counselling and physiotherapy qualifications, I don't need to add the medical stuff.'

'That makes no sense—and then there's the small issue of your name.'

'You're treating me like a criminal.'

'You're acting like one.'

'It's not a sin to change your name.'

'People don't change their names unless they're hiding.'

'So I'm hiding, but my reasons are personal and nothing to do with my professional ability. I ask you to accept that.'

'So if I ring the medical board and enquire…'

'I'd ask you not to do that.' Her face was pale but resolute. She stood halfway up the steps, holding onto the rail as if she needed it for support. 'I've taken a great deal of trouble to ensure there's no link between Cathy Heineman and Kate Martin. One phone call could destroy that. One phone call could mean I need to walk away from all I've worked for.'

'You mean the medical board—'

'Couldn't care less,' she snapped. 'I have my change of name recorded. Believe it or not, I'm still a registered doctor with no blemish against my name. I still accrue my professional training points and I keep my registration up to date. But the receptionist who receives notes of my continual professional training updates Kate Martin's file. I did the name change carefully with only a couple of trusted friends helping. I want no link.'

There were a couple of moments of silence. Intense silence. She was gazing straight up at him, unflinching. Defiant even. Still, she was pale.

One phone call could mean I need to walk away from all I've worked for...

This was personal, he thought. He shouldn't ask.

But this was Harry.

'Cathy...Kate,' he said at last. 'Harry's lost his parents. He has no one to protect him except me and his very bossy aunt. Helen demanded that I bring him here. I did so with reservations because alternative medicine makes me wary, and the first thing I saw was a dead child. That was followed by a doctor using an assumed name. Your defensiveness might be valid from your perspective but for Harry's sake I need an explanation.'

'You can't just let Maisie and the dolphins do their own work without probing into my past?'

'No,' he said flatly. 'Harry's too important for that.'

'You were my friend,' she said. 'You trusted me.'

'I trusted you not to break a test tube,' he said. 'And they were the university's test tubes. This is Harry.'

She bit her lip. Her gaze faltered for a moment. She stared down at her bare toes and then she raised her chin again. She met his gaze with that same defiance, but touched with the defiance was a hint of fear.

'I don't tell people.'

'No.'

'Can I trust you?'

'You can trust me not to tell anyone else. You can't trust me not to pick up Harry and walk away.'

'Fair enough.' She sighed and then seemed to come to a decision. 'There's wine in your refrigerator. I'm off duty. If I don't charge you mini-bar prices, will you pour me one? You can have a free beer as well.'

'Bribing as well?' he asked, but he smiled to soften the words and she managed a smile back.

'I'll do anything I need to stay hidden,' she said simply. 'Handing you access to your mini-bar is the least of it.'

She was settled in the deck chair on Jack's veranda. Jack had nearly finished his beer and she was halfway through a glass of wine.

She'd expected him to push, but he didn't. He seemed content to wait, giving her the time she needed.

And she needed time. Her story was simple and bleak and it was something that had happened to a woman called Cathy Heineman, not to her. She was Kate Martin and she'd moved on.

But Jack was still waiting. If he was to trust her, he had a right to know.

'You know I married,' she said.

'I did know that.'

'Fourth year. I was twenty-one. A kid.'

'We seemed pretty old and wise at the time.'

'We did, didn't we?' she said, and tried for a smile. 'But I was still a baby. Still living at home, the only child of elderly parents. Ruled by a loving despot. My father's health was precarious and my mother was terrified. Dad had two heart attacks while I was in my teens, and Mum's mantra was *Don't do anything to upset your father.*'

'So?'

'So that was the way it was,' she said. 'Simon was the son of Dad's best friend and business partner. Almost family. I was sixteen when we first dated. Simon was twenty four and the excitement our parents felt was amazing. The assumption from that first date was that we'd marry.'

'But you obviously liked the guy.'

'Oh, yes. But he was just...an extension of my family. He was older than me, good looking, powerful, and he fed my teenage ego no end. And suddenly I was in too far to get out. When I started university I started getting itchy feet, but by then Dad's health was failing even more. The pressure was on for us to marry before he died. Simon was pressuring me too, saying he was fond of my dad, we should do it. So I did.'

She said it almost defiantly, as if it was a thing that needed defending.

He stayed silent. There was more coming; he knew it.

'Only, of course, then I was a wife,' she said slowly. 'Before I'd been a girlfriend, almost a casual girlfriend as Simon had let me go my own way—as indeed he went his. He was training to take over our parents' business. He was an only child too, so we'd both inherit and the business—importing quality wine—was brilliant. Both families were wealthy, but Simon wanted more.'

'Is that why he married you?' Jack asked.

Kate stared into her wine glass for a long moment before she answered. Then: 'Yes,' she said. 'Of course it was, only I was too naïve to see it. All I saw was that he was a nice guy, and my father was desperate for the marriage. I think...maybe even then I was thinking if it doesn't work out, after Dad and Mum go I can divorce. I was only twenty one. I had my medical career to get off the ground. I didn't intend to have babies for years.'

'But?' he said gently, and she swirled her wine some more.

'But,' she said heavily. 'But.'

'If you don't want to tell me, I can get the picture.'

She glanced up at him then and managed a smile. 'So little, and you'll trust?'

'I assume you're running from him?'

'See, in his eyes I'm not Cathy or Kate,' she told

him. 'Divorce or not, I'm his wife. I'm the other part of Simon's inheritance, and Simon doesn't give up possessions lightly.'

'I see.'

'You probably don't. The fights we had… First he wanted me to give up my medical studies. After we married he couldn't see the point. I fought him on that, you can't believe how much I fought, and I won but at a cost. And after that…every little thing meant a fight. If I defied him, heaven help me. He wanted total control. And then Dad died, Simon's father went into care with Alzheimer's and the whole thing crashed.' She faltered. 'It seemed… Simon gambled. No one knew. No one suspected. But he'd mortgaged the business. He'd forged signatures so my half as well as his was forfeit. I knew then why he'd married me and I knew why he had to stay married. But after one vicious fight too many I walked away, and then, after what happened next, I ran.'

'Cathy—'

'I'm Kate,' she said fiercely. 'I'm Kate Martin. Cathy Heineman is divorced and has disappeared because Simon still thinks he owns her. Simon went to jail because he signed contracts using my mother's name and mine. My mother died in poverty because of him. His own parents are penniless. Simon is a lying, thieving thug and I'm glad my parents are dead because they never had to see…'

She caught herself. 'No. It's not necessary to tell you all the gruesome facts. Just that I didn't take forgery and theft lying down. It wasn't just me he robbed but I was the one who sent him to jail. So Simon still hates me and he's lethal. Ten years on, he's been in and out of jail and I'm still afraid of him. His hatred is out of all context, off the wall. So I'm Kate. I changed my name. I scraped together enough from our assets to go overseas.

I worked as a waitress while I retrained as a physiothera-pist. I did some psychology too—in some ways it helped with the stuff that had happened to me. The university in Auckland was supportive. My medical degree meant additional qualifications were fast-tracked and I quali-fied with my new name.

'Then I heard about this place. Even though it was back in Australia, a dolphin sanctuary three hundred miles from the nearest city seemed perfect. I can vet cli-ents before taking bookings. If there's a familiar name I can say we're full up, as we nearly always are. It's only because Harry was booked in under his aunt's name that I missed you.'

'And your qualifications?' he asked. 'Why don't you advertise your medical degree?'

'I know Simon,' she said. 'He'll suspect I've changed my name. I wouldn't put it past him to check every doc-tor on the medical register, here and in New Zealand. You see,' she said simply, 'I'm still afraid of him.'

'No man has the right—'

'He has no rights,' she said flatly. 'But neither does he have reason. Somehow my lovely, smart divorce law-yer managed to scrape back enough money for me to re-train, but it took criminal charges to do it. Even though I didn't throw half the charges I could have at him, he's never forgiven me. But that's enough,' she said, moving on. 'That's all the explanation I can give, so accept it or not. I think I can help Harry. Today's reaction to Maisie says we can reach him. I believe swimming with the dol-phins, one on one, will help him enormously but it's up to you. I won't push. Leave in the morning if you want—all I ask is that you keep my confidence. Will you do that?'

'Of course I will.'

Of course.

He thought back to the friend he'd had at university.

Cathy had been a lovely, laughing girl whose humour had made lab work fun. She'd had her intense side but none of them had ever suspected she'd had such shadows.

Cathy was now Kate, he thought. She was a different woman, but underneath she must be the same.

Would he let her treat Harry? With her explanation, and after Harry's reaction to the events of today, it was a no-brainer.

'Let me show you Toby's notes,' she said, and he stilled.

'Toby...'

'You're Harry's guardian. I saw the way you reacted to Toby's death and I don't blame you. I need...for myself...to reassure you that everything that could be done was done.'

'It's not my business. There's no need—'

'There is a need,' she said. 'And I have Amy's permission. Her sister and her mum are here to help her take Toby back to Sydney. She's overwhelmed, but she still registered your shock on the beach. I told her you were a doctor. She said...' She swallowed, fighting for composure. 'She told me to do whatever I must to persuade you to let me help Harry. So here you are.' And she tugged a sheaf of medical notes and X-rays from the envelope and handed them over.

He glanced through them. There was no need for questions: they spoke for themselves. As an oncologist, Jack had treated brain tumours—of course he had. Even the sight of the first X-ray, before surgery, before chemotherapy, had him knowing the end had been inevitable. The surgery and chemotherapy had been acts of desperation, buying a little time but not much.

Resuscitation today would have been stupid and cruel. That this little boy had died where he had seemed little short of a miracle.

He stared at the films, at the notes, at the final letter from an oncologist he knew, saying take him home and love him, and he felt his chest tighten.

He'd so nearly intervened. If he'd come moments before…

'I wouldn't have let you interfere,' Kate said simply, watching his face. 'I'm in control here, and I don't make decisions lightly. I do what's best for each of my clients. I'll do what's best for Harry.'

'I believe you.' There was nothing else to say.

'And I promise I won't let Maisie trick you again,' she said, and the tension broke.

He gathered the notes and put them back into their envelope. It gave him time to collect himself, even drum up a smile. 'She's a smart dog.'

'I found her as a pup. Believe it or not, someone threw her from a car. She was past the cute puppy stage so someone dumped her, scraggy and half-starved. I'd just accepted the job here and this place is a wildlife sanctuary, no pets allowed. The powers that be had to be talked into letting me keep her but they really wanted my combination of qualifications so they bent the rules. Now there's not a soul who's not totally devoted to her. Sometimes I think I'm not even needed. Maisie treats the kids for me.'

'As well as tricking parents.'

'She's discovered it makes kids laugh,' she said simply. 'What sort of gift is that?'

'Beyond price.'

She beamed, lighting up. Serious confidences over. 'Exactly. So you will stay?'

'I… Yes.'

'Excellent,' she said, and motioned to the second envelope. 'Let's get this done, then. Forms. Questions. I need to know all about Harry, and all about you.'

'Me?'

'Are you Harry's legal guardian?'

'Yes.'

'Will he live with you full time when he leaves here?'

He hesitated. There was a huge question. It was one he'd been asking himself over and over.

He was a bachelor, nicely confirmed. He was also an oncologist and a busy one. He had a girlfriend but theirs was long-term semi-commitment. Their lifestyle suited them both.

He and Annalise were ambitious. Neither wanted to be tied down—apartments in the same luxury block was as close as either wanted to get. Annalise had her life and he had his.

Where would Harry fit?

'Earth to Jack,' Kate said, and he realised he'd been staring out over the sea for too long.

'I don't know,' he said at last. 'If you can cure him, maybe he can live with his Aunt Helen. She's a mother hen. She has five kids and would like more.'

'Define cure,' she said. 'What are you hoping for?'

'He's so withdrawn.'

'Some kids *are* withdrawn. Was he like that when his parents were alive?'

'He was quiet,' he conceded.

'You love him?'

'He's my nephew.'

'It doesn't necessarily follow that you love him.'

'I loved my sister,' he said inconsequentially, and she nodded.

'I'm sorry.'

'He's very like her.'

'Quiet.'

'Not so much quiet as observant. My sister noticed everything. So does...so did Harry.'

'But not now.'

'He doesn't say.'

'The original form we received said he was living with his aunt.'

'It's a good home.' Why did he suddenly feel like he was stuck on a pin, like an impaled butterfly? 'They have a huge house. Helen's great with kids, and so's her husband. Harry should be happy there.'

'But he's not.'

'He just...disappears. Shrinks. I can't explain it.'

'So you want me to make him outgoing and boisterous so he'll fit into a family of five kids. It won't happen,' she said bluntly. 'A family of five has their own pecking order, their own entrenched hierarchy. To put a wounded seven-year-old in their midst will never work.'

'He won't be wounded. If I can just get him talking...'

'He's lost his parents,' Kate said flatly. 'He'll always be wounded.'

This wasn't what he wanted to hear, but he stared out to sea some more and he knew it was the truth. Harry was never going to fit in with Helen's brood. So where did that leave him?

'Do you have a wife or partner?' Kate asked, not without sympathy.

'Um...yes. Girlfriend.' Maybe not partner. They weren't close enough for that.

'One who likes kids?'

'No. Not that I'm planning to palm him off—'

'I'm not saying you are. It's just that kids are hard work. Taking on a seven-year-old is huge. If you and...'

'Annalise,' he said, and he knew he sounded goaded but he couldn't help it. The sensation of being impaled was growing.

'Annalise,' she said. 'Nice name. If you and Annalise plan on having babies of your own it'll make things more complicated.'

'This isn't about me.'

'Of course it's about you. Harry's whole future seems to be about you.'

This wasn't what he wanted to hear. 'Look, can we get tomorrow over with first?'

'You're definitely staying tomorrow?'

'Yes.'

'But you haven't made your mind up about after that? Whether you're ready to be Harry's dad?'

'I'll be Harry's guardian.'

'That's not enough. Harry needs more and you know it. If Annalise isn't interested, you'll be Harry's mum and dad combined.'

'Will you leave it?' It was an explosion in the stillness of the night, startling him as well as the couple of bush turkeys scratching at the footings of the bungalow. 'It'll sort itself out as we go along.'

'Does Harry know where his future lies?'

'What do you mean?'

'I mean Harry's been in hospital and then at his Aunt Helen's with his five cousins and then travelling with you and now he's here. Does he have any idea where he's going to live; what his future life will be like?'

'What business—?'

'Is it of mine? Plenty. This isn't just a place where kids come to play with dolphins. The dolphins are background. What they do is help the kids relax so we can help them sort the problems surrounding them. We achieve therapeutic success because our environment is far less threatening than any normal medical setting. As well as that, the dolphins—and Maisie—actively remove barriers wounded kids put up around themselves. They forget to defend themselves. I'm willing to bet we can get

Harry doing more with his legs tomorrow than he's done since the accident. As well as that, he'll be more receptive to talking. But, Jack, what Harry needs right now is certainty and that's up to you.'

She rose and laid the forms down on the table. 'These forms aren't just about you,' she said. 'They're about you and Harry. The mending team. The family. You need to work it out so that when Harry surfaces from grief and shock and manages to ask, you can give him the assurances he needs. Mind, it'd be better if you could give him those assurances now, but you have things to come to terms with as well. If you like, we'll organise you your own dolphin companion to help. Meanwhile, can you fill these forms in for me? I'll pick them up in the morning.'

She turned to go but then she hesitated, turning back.

'Jack, thank you for reassuring me about my name change,' she said softly. 'It means everything to me. And thank you also for entrusting Harry to my care. I will help. I promise.'

'I know you will.' Where had that come from? But he knew it was true. From total distrust, he now had faith.

Why? Because she told a good story? Because he'd known her as a student? Because she was forcing him to face something he'd been actively avoiding?

Or maybe it was none of those things. Maybe it was because she was standing in the moonlight in her faded jeans and windcheater and her bare feet, and she looked about fourteen, although he knew she was much older.

Maybe it was the freckles.

Maybe it was the smile. She was smiling now, quizzically, waiting for him to say goodnight and give her leave to go.

'Won't you have another drink?' he found himself saying.

She looked at him then, really looked, and he was reminded of the looks she'd given him when he'd been fooling round in the lab at med school, when time had been starting to run out and she'd reminded him they were there to work. And he remembered suddenly how much he'd wanted to ask her out, and how frustrated he'd been when she'd knocked back his advances.

But she wasn't thinking about the past. This was all about now. This was all about Harry.

'This is my job,' she told him gently. 'Jack, you're the parent of my client. I might have sand between my toes but here I'm every inch a professional. I had a glass of wine with you then because I needed to break that professionalism to gain your trust, but now we need to move forward. Besides,' she said gently, and she even managed a bit of a teasing grin, 'Annalise wouldn't like it. Goodnight, Jack.'

And she was gone, slipping silently into the shadows, leaving him with the forms to be filled in, with the moonlight over the sea and with silence.

And with all the questions in the world racing through his head.

Inside Harry was asleep, curled up with a great lump of a trickster dog. He was seven years old and totally dependent on him.

Back at Sydney Central, Annalise would be expecting a call.

But it was Friday night. On Friday nights he and friends usually went out to Silence, a discreet and expensive supper club where great jazz was played, where excellent wines were served, where medics could unwind after the tensions of the week. And spend a lot of money.

Annalise would be there now, he thought, enjoying herself even without him. She'd be looking beautiful, tall, willowy, blonde, dressed simply but flawlessly. She'd be laughing, sparkling, the centre of attention. If he phoned her now she'd step out onto the balcony and watch the harbour lights while she talked sympathetically to him about what he was doing. Then she'd step back into his world.

How could he take Harry back there?

He was here to fix him and prepare him for entry into Helen's family. That had been his hope but now the plan seemed...flawed?

Why? Because a wounded and hunted doctor with bare feet and a freckled nose had told him it was flawed?

And why were those freckles superimposing themselves over Annalise's more glamorous image?

It was because he was tired, he told himself, and also because he was shocked. He thought back to the Cathy he'd known during med school—and he thought of how she'd changed after she'd married. She'd withdrawn into herself. They'd all noticed it but none of them had pushed to find out why.

They'd been kids. They'd been centred on passing final exams. The thought that any one of them could be in an abusive relationship had been so far out of their ken that it had been unthinkable.

Yet he'd thought of himself as her friend, and he'd never asked. He'd never pushed to know about this unknown husband. Maybe he'd even been a bit resentful that she'd clearly preferred someone else. Adolescent jealousy? How dumb was that?

But it was no use feeling guilty now, he told himself. As Cathy...Kate had said, from now on this was a professional relationship. He was here to cure Harry.

Cure?

Tonight Kate—and he would think of her as Kate, he conceded, because professionalism was the only way to face the next few days—had reminded him that Harry was still the same Harry he'd always been underneath his shock and grief and battering. She'd forced him to acknowledge that a quiet, shy little boy was always going to be quiet and shy and that maybe he'd never fit in with Helen's brood.

Which left him where?

He thought of his sister, Beth. She'd also been quiet and shy. She'd been his little sister and he'd loved her.

She'd want him to look after her little boy. Of course she would. But how?

He thought back to the supper club, to where he should be now and where he wanted to be again. Then he looked out to sea.

A burst of fluorescence broke the trail of silver moonlight over the water as a dolphin leaped high, curved and plunged into the depths again. It was no wonder people associated dolphins with magic, he thought. Here in the moonlight it was almost possible to believe they were right.

Which was nonsense. He had to stay practical.

The problem was that his problem had got past the practical. It was so immense it needed a little magic.

Kate had found peace here, he thought inconsequentially. She'd found a new life. She'd found a solution. Maybe...

Or maybe not. This place was a temporary refuge. The real world was waiting. He'd take Harry back and try and figure out a future.

As Kate had.

Why was he still thinking of her? Weren't his own problems paramount?

Maybe they were. He poured himself another beer but he didn't drink it. Instead, he stared at the sea, unconsciously willing another dolphin to break the surface.

It didn't. It seemed the magic was over for the night.

It was time to head for bed, get rested ready for whatever tomorrow held.

It was time to stop thinking about a woman who'd changed her name from Cathy to Kate.

Kate walked back to her own little bungalow behind the administration building and prepared for bed. Today had been gut-wrenching. As much as she'd been prepared for Toby's death... No, nothing *ever* prepared you for a child's death. It had cut deep, and then, as she'd been still struggling to control her emotions, Jack Kincaid had walked back into her life.

Jack. Big, larger than life, smart, funny, nice. At med school she'd thought of him as one of her best friends, and after her marriage she'd struggled to withdraw from his friendship.

She shouldn't have had to withdraw but Simon's jealousy had been stretched to the limit coping with her desire to do medicine. For her to have an outside circle of friends had been something she'd had to sacrifice.

She should have walked away so much sooner. That first week of her marriage, on their honeymoon, Simon had left her at dinner to make a telephone call. A fellow diner had approached her and started chatting. Yes, it had been a come-on, yes, she had been dressed up to the nines, alone, female, and Simon's long telephone call had left her looking stranded.

But on his return Simon's reaction had been icy. He'd cut the guy dead, and for the rest of the night and the next day Kate had been 'punished'. Lesson: 'You want me to love you, then you're mine and mine alone. I'm in control.'

She should have walked. No, she should have run, but her parents would have been heartbroken and, besides, Simon had been lovely underneath—hadn't he? When he'd been happy he could make her happy. She'd just had to be careful.

How long until she'd been totally under his control? How long until she'd finally snapped out of it and realised how much of a victim she'd become?

It had taken a hysterical phone call from her mother— 'He's taken everything.' Bleak to the bottom of her soul, she'd gone to the police. Not just with evidence of fraud but with resolution as cold as ice.

Then…months in a women's refuge. Help from the wonderful women who ran these places. Help from the police—it seemed his family wasn't alone in the list of people Simon had cheated.

What had followed had been a name change and a move to New Zealand. A new life. Even a sort of peace, though trust in herself was still hard to come by.

And then today here was Jack, bringing memories of a time when she'd still been Cathy, when life had been fun, when the most important thing in the world hadn't been to hide.

Jack…

She'd always thought he was gorgeous, she reflected, but, of course, even in first year she'd already had Simon as her permanent boyfriend. She'd been able to watch from the sidelines and tease as he'd gone through his myriad girlfriends. Jack had treated life as one long game, though in his medicine that game had been used to effect. He'd never lost sight of his patients' needs, and his laughter had been used to make them smile.

He'd lost his sister now and his smile had faded but it was still there behind the grief. There was still Annalise in the background. He was struggling with his little nephew's needs, but he'd manage, he'd juggle, he'd call in favours, he'd get what he wanted.

Would he commit to Harry?

It couldn't matter to her, she decided. She'd do what she could for the time they were here and then see them leave. What was it they'd taught her in medical school all those years ago? Don't judge. Accept people for what they are, do what you can for them but in the end their choices are their own.

Don't...care?

Impossible.

She wouldn't mind if Maisie was here.

Maybe she should get another dog, she thought, now Maisie had taken it on herself to divide her loyalty between the kids she loved playing with during the day. But, then, a puppy would be adored by the kids as well, so she'd have two dogs out comforting kids. She wouldn't mind a bit of comfort herself.

'Wuss.' She'd said it out loud and it echoed in the quiet of the bungalow.

She thought back to those first few dreadful weeks of sleeping in the women's refuge. She'd lain in bed at night and she'd formed a mantra.

'I don't need anyone. I'm worth something in my own right and I can live alone.'

She'd been saying that to herself for years now and she believed it. Or she almost believed it.

Right now she'd like Maisie.

And, stupidly or not, right now she couldn't stop thinking of Jack.

CHAPTER FOUR

JACK WOKE TO a whump, whump, whump out in the living room. He opened one eye and peered out. Maisie was sitting at the front door, her big tail thumping with anticipation. She obviously wanted out.

Harry was standing beside her, looking worried.

He should get up and let her out, but after a moment's thought he decided against it. He closed his eyes again. Apart from the couple of outbursts yesterday when the excitement had been too much for him, Harry had retreated to silence, but here was another situation where silence might not work.

So he lay and waited while the thumping grew increasingly excited. Harry's indecision was practically vibrating through the bungalow.

And finally Harry cracked. Jack lay silent as he heard footsteps approach, as a small hand landed on his shoulder.

'Uncle Jack,' Harry said, and that was a breakthrough all by itself.

'Call me Jack,' Jack growled, still without opening his eyes. He'd already figured 'uncle' was a barrier. *'Harry, do what Auntie Helen tells you. Harry, go and play with your cousin Alice.'* Titles were a barrier he could do without.

'Jack,' Harry whispered, and Jack opened his eyes,

but sleepily, like there was all the time in the world and it was no big deal that Harry had called him by name.

'Morning,' he said. 'Is the sun up?'

'Everyone's up,' Harry whispered. 'Everyone's on the beach. Maisie wants to go. Should I let her out?'

'Is Kate on the beach?'

'Y-yes.'

'Then let her out but leave the door open so we can watch her. After breakfast we'll go down and see if Kate wants her. If not, we'll go down and bring her back.'

Brilliant. Kate knew what she was doing, leaving Maisie with him for the night. Left to his own devices, Harry would have stayed in bed, and there'd be no way he'd go to the beach unless propelled. But like yesterday, Maisie had done Kate's propelling for her.

Back in Sydney Jack had thought of this place disparagingly. It had seemed an alternative therapy of dubious repute. But right here, right now, it looked okay. This wasn't 'alternative'. This was working.

And Harry ate, not a huge amount but enough to keep Jack satisfied, and instead of needing encouragement at every mouthful Harry had obviously decided how much Jack would let him get away with and shovelled it in fast. Dog. Beach. Go.

Just as Harry gulped the last of his juice Kate arrived, Maisie loping along behind her. She was wearing her stinger suit again. Her hair was twisted into a knot on the top of her head, she had rock sandals on her feet and she looked about as far from a doctor as it was possible to get.

'I thought you might like swim gear,' she said cheerfully. The suits were probably the most unattractive garments in the planet but she held them out like they were gold. 'These mean you don't need to use sunscreen.'

'Are there stingers in the water?' Jack asked, and then

could have bitten his tongue. The last thing he wanted was to scare Harry.

But Kate was grinning. 'No. They're like school uniform, meant to make everyone here equal. Socialists R Us.' Then, at Harry's look of confusion, she stooped to talk only to him. Her body language was obvious. Her client was Harry. Jack was just a bystander.

'Later this morning I'd like to take you to meet the dolphins close up,' she told him. 'And dolphins don't like sunscreen. Kids like you go into their pool every day. If everyone had sunscreen on, it'd float off and stick to the dolphins. Then none of them would get a tan and we'd have a whole pod of pure white dolphins. Maybe they'd get freckles, just like me. So we all wear blue suits to stop dolphin freckles.'

Harry gazed at her in confusion. And then, very slowly, as if something was cracking inside, he managed a wavery smile.

'That's silly.'

'Yep, I'm always silly,' she admitted. 'But, seriously, dolphins don't like sunscreen; it's not good for them. Harry, I have two little girls I need to see before I can spend time with you. Dianne and Ross, our play therapists, are playing with a beachball down by the waves. You can join in, or you and your Uncle Jack can build a sandcastle or paddle or swim or do whatever you want.'

'He's Jack,' Harry whispered, and it was so low Jack could hardly hear. But he heard, for he was listening like it was the most important message he could hear. 'He likes us calling him Jack.'

'Of course,' Kate said, and finally that smile was directed at him. 'Okay, Jack and Harry, put your swimsuits on and go and have fun. And don't let Maisie fool you again—Jack.'

'No one's fooling anyone,' Jack said, and smiled back at her, and thought what the heck did he mean?

He didn't have a clue. All he knew was that he was off to build sandcastles.

On the beach Harry retreated again into silence. That was okay for Jack didn't need to do anything about it. Maisie had things under control. The big dog sat by Harry's side for a while, giving him time to get accustomed, and then suddenly she started digging. Harry looked astonished. Maisie dug some more, sand spraying everywhere, then sat on her haunches and looked at Harry. Harry looked back.

Maisie dug again, sand sprayed everywhere, then she sat on her haunches again and looked at Harry. Harry resisted.

Maisie dug even more, sand sprayed everywhere, then she sat on her haunches and looked at Harry some more.

Enough.

Harry dug.

Jack hadn't been aware he'd been holding his breath, but it came out now in a rush. He looked up and one of the therapists was giving him a discreet thumbs-up sign.

How had they persuaded Maisie to do that? Who knew? But he was profoundly grateful.

Pressure off, he sat back and watched the whole scene.

The play beach was distant from the enclosed dolphin pool and Jack could see why. In the distance he could see Kate with a couple and a child. Therapy? He couldn't tell; they were far enough away to ensure privacy.

The two therapists on the beach, Dianne and Ross, were working hard but they were like big kids. Dianne was a woman in her forties, Ross was practically a teenager but dressed in their standard-issue blue suits they seemed of an age. They mixed happily with kids and parents, gently encouraging kids to mix and play, but they didn't push. They made it seem like the most natural thing in the world to join in and have fun.

But they didn't push Harry. He was left to his digging. There were a couple of other kids who stayed back, and that was okay, too. A couple of times the beach ball just 'happened' to fly in their direction and the therapists swooped to retrieve it, thanking the individual child as if they'd retrieved it themselves.

No pressure.

' Jack looked around at this motley group of parents and children. Some were overtly injured, scarred, frail. Some must be emotionally injured for there were no outward signs of what was wrong, but he'd seen the application forms. The only kids here were those whose need was strong.

And for the first time since he'd had the phone call saying his sister was dead, he found himself feeling calm. Helen had been right: this was a good place for Harry to be.

He could relax. Someone else was doing the worrying for him.

Harry was digging his way to China.

The therapists were playing keepings off, swooping off along the beach with a ragtag of children following.

There was a stir just behind him, a cry. He turned and a woman was struggling to hold a child, a girl about twelve or thirteen.

She was arching back in her mother's arms, and her involuntary jerks told Jack she was in mid-convulsion.

Harry stared. 'Jack,' he breathed, and this, too, was amazing. Not only had he registered something was wrong, he was expecting Jack to do something about it.

Kate was in the water. The therapists were far down

the beach, chasing children. With his medical training, Jack certainly needed to do something about it.

The child was only ten yards away and he reached her fast, kneeling on the sand, automatically starting to check her airway as the woman with her tried to hold her still.

Toby's death yesterday was front and foremost in his mind. Another brain tumour? How many seriously ill children did Kate have here?

But it was no such thing. 'It's all right,' the woman managed. 'It's... Susie's epileptic. She won't take...I thought she'd taken but she hates...and she hates people seeing.'

'I'm a doctor,' Jack told her. 'Let me help.'

The kid was an almost-teen, Jack thought, automatically taking her from her mother's arms and shifting her sideways. As an oncologist he treated kids of this age, and he understood their trauma. Sometimes the side effects of their illness seemed more terrible to the kids than the illness itself. Hair loss. Hospitalisation and enforced distance from their peer group. Being seen as different. *Different*. A fate worse than death for a teenager.

'Put the beach towel down for me,' he told the woman, and once again got a shock as Harry moved to help. The girl was rigid, arching, breathing noisily and seemingly unaware of her surroundings. If she was indeed epileptic, though, all they needed to do was keep her safe until the convulsion passed.

He set her down, rolling her onto her side. Then checked his watch. Convulsions always seemed to last for ever. There was no need to worry if it didn't go past five minutes but, watching a kid convulse, it was very hard to register time.

'My husband's gone to make a phone call for work,' the woman sobbed. 'He's with the police; they're always calling him, even though he's supposed to be here, help-

ing me care. And I don't know what to do. I never do. I
hate these attacks. Don's better than me with coping. I
can't… Should I call someone? Kate?'

But Jack had been here before, all too often. His little
sister had been epileptic.… *Both* his parents had hated
her attacks. Jack had learned to cope early, and his medical training had reinforced what he'd learned the hard
way. The only thing Beth had hated more than her epileptic attacks had been people seeing her having them,
and this kid would be no different. He glanced across
at Kate and then along the beach to the therapists. Any
call would make everyone on the beach aware of what
was happening.

His body was blocking the view for the moment and
no one else seemed to have noticed. If they could keep
this private…

'I'm sure I can look after her,' he told Susie's mum.
'There's no problem. Harry, can you give me a hand to
shift these two beach shelters so we can get some shade?'

It wasn't shade they needed. The beach was only pleas-
antly warm. But Harry was only too eager to help. They
hauled two of the little shelters around so they made a
V, the opening looking out to the water. It effectively
blocked off anyone along the beach seeing, but it looked
like he'd simply hauled two shelters together so two families could chat.

Then he settled beside her, checked her airway again,
checked her pulse, kept watch. And as Harry looked un-
sure, he tugged him down so the little boy was on his
knee.

'This looks a lot scarier than it is,' he told Harry, and
as he talked, Susie's body lost some of her rigidity. Her
mum was stroking her face, making sure her hair was out
of her eyes, keeping watch as Jack was doing. The girl's
eyes flickered open and registered her mum.

'I'm Dr Jack,' Jack told her, pretty sure she couldn't take it in yet, but he'd reassure her anyway. 'And no one can see.'

'What's wrong?' Harry breathed.

'It's called epilepsy,' Jack said, keeping his voice even and strong, knowing his presence would be reassuring the mother, if not the teen. 'But it's okay. Lots of people have it. When you watch television, do you ever notice that occasionally the picture goes fuzzy for a minute or you get funny lines? Only for a minute and then it goes back to normal.'

'Yes,' Harry said, cautiously.

'Well, that's what epilepsy is,' Jack said. 'It's like a little electronic signal in Susie's brain gets the wrong signals. It's called a tonic-clonic seizure. That's a long name for something that's usually very short. Susie's waking up now. She'll be back to being herself in no time.'

They sat on. Susie was gradually returning to normal. He watched as her eyes lost their dazed, faraway look, focussed, cringed.

'It's okay,' he said, as her focus returned. 'A momentary hiccup that no one saw.'

'Th-thank you.' Susie's mum was still close to tears, but Jack gave her a warning look. The last thing Susie needed now was emotion.

She was curling into herself, a fragile kid on the edge of womanhood. Her clinging stinger suit showed the faint budding of breasts. Her brown hair was tugged back into a glittery band, and if he wasn't mistaken she had a touch of make-up on under the sunscreen on her nose.

He remembered Beth at that age. It hurt to remember her.

'My sister had epilepsy,' he heard himself say and he hadn't meant to say it until it came out. 'Beth.'

'My...my Mum,' Harry whispered.

'That's right.'

'She never looked like Susie looked.'

'That's because she had control of her medication,' Jack said. 'She never missed. Do you remember, Harry, that your mum took pills every breakfast-time?'

'She was old,' Susie managed. 'It'd be okay if…I was old.'

Jack winced. The thought of Beth as old was unthinkable but, then, at thirteen, even twenty probably seemed ancient.

'Beth had epilepsy from when she was a baby,' Jack said. 'It wasn't serious. The only time it was a problem was when she was a teenager and she thought the pills made her gain weight.'

And Susie stilled. Bingo, Jack thought, glancing at Susie's mum. Teenagers worrying about body image. Some things were perennial.

'She tried not taking her medication,' Jack said. 'That was a disaster. She had seizures at school and the kids saw her and that seemed to make things worse. Finally, though, she figured she might control her weight gain with exercise. She got her black belt for karate. After that no one messed with my sister, ever again, and she was beautiful.'

'But…what happened to her?' Susie seemed wide awake now, aware, even glancing at Harry. 'Is that… his…mum?'

'Beth was Harry's mum,' he agreed. 'She and Harry's dad were killed in a car accident. It had nothing to do with her epilepsy, though, Susie—a drunk driver crashed into the family car. Before that…she had a great life. She went to uni, had fun, met a gorgeous boy and married him, had Harry. Nothing stopped her.'

'I don't…I don't like karate,' Susie managed, and Jack had to suppress a smile. Harry's tragedy, Beth's death were taking a back seat to Susie's problems. Of course they were. Could any adolescent be different?

'Sports come in all shapes and sizes,' he told her. He glanced out at the sea. 'What about swimming? Do you like swimming with the dolphins?'

'Yeah, but...' She hesitated, licking her lips, and Jack knew she'd still be struggling with the feeling of coming out of the fog. Her mouth would be thick and dry, she needed fluids, then rest with quiet. But for some reason instinct told him he should go along with this conversation. 'I wanted to dance,' she whispered, and he knew he was right.

'So why don't you?'

'She had an episode at dance class last year,' her mum said. 'The girls...weren't very kind.'

'Ouch. Other girls can be horrid at your age,' Jack said bluntly. 'Beth used to complain about them, too. But she never let them stop her. Do you know that one person in every fifty is an epileptic? Two people in every hundred. So I'm willing to bet that some of the most famous dancers in the world are epileptic.'

'They can't be,' Susie breathed.

'Want to bet?' Jack demanded. 'Tell you what, if I'm wrong I'll let all the kids bury me up to my neck in sand and leave me there for an hour. But I bet I'm right. I have my computer here, and a printer. I'll look it up tonight and I'll have a list of dancers who have epilepsy sitting on your doorstep tomorrow.'

'You're...silly,' Susie managed.

'He is.' Harry beamed. Finally, here was something he agreed with. 'Jack's silly.'

'And I hope he's not bothering you.' It was Kate; of course it was Kate. How long had she been there, on the other side of the screens, listening and waiting for a chance to break in? He tugged back the screen and she was calmly sitting on the sand, with Maisie's head in her lap, as if this was where she sat all the time. 'Jack's an excellent doctor but he can be silly,' she told Susie, as if she'd been part of the conversation all along. But there was no mention of what had just happened. No fuss. 'I went to university with him,' she told Susie. 'So I should know.'

'He says I can still dance,' Susie faltered.

'Then make him prove it.'

'He says he will. I…hope.'

'Then, silly or not, if he says he will then he will,' Kate said, smiled down at Susie. 'You feeling okay now?'

'I… Yes.'

'Not too fuzzy-headed to swim with the dolphins this afternoon?'

'No!'

'Maybe a wee rest first?'

'Okay.'

'Great,' Kate said, and moved on, as if the whole episode was behind them.

'How did you know what happened?' Jack demanded, as Susie and her mum made their way back to the bungalows, walking hand in hand as if nothing had happened.

'I saw,' Kate said. 'I was about to come up but then you took over. Thank you.'

'You're welcome.' He hesitated. 'How many medical problems do you have in this place?'

'More now that I'm here,' she said. 'We don't advertise medical care, but now I'm here we don't turn away kids with conditions like Toby's. But Susie doesn't need medical care. She just needs…confidence.' She smiled down at Harry. 'And, Harry, your Jack might be silly but he did a great job looking after Susie. He said just the right thing. I'm grateful.'

What was there in that to make a man want to blush? Nothing. It was a simple compliment, nothing more. But Kate's smile transferred itself to him and he definitely wanted to blush. Or something.

That smile had stayed the same since the first time he'd met her.

That smile was really something.

'You want to meet the dolphins now?' Kate asked Harry, and the moment was broken. But not the sensation. Not the desire to see more of that smile.

Harry hesitated but Maisie had leaped to attention and her whole body quivered. She looked from Harry to Kate and back again, and her message couldn't be clearer.

There's fun this way. Come with me and play.

How did they train a dog to do this?

No matter, the message was irresistible. Harry put a tentative hand on Maisie's collar and it was like pressing a go button. Maisie headed off steadily along the beach with Kate, with Harry clinging behind.

Bemused, Jack was left to follow.

He walked slowly, watching Kate chat to his nephew. Down at the water two of the dolphins were playing with a ball, tossing it seemingly just for pleasure. The sun was glittering on the sea, the tiny waves were only knee high at most and sandpipers were once again searching for pippies along the shoreline. This was the most perfect place.

'You're welcome to join us but you don't have to come in with us, Jack,' Kate said, quite kindly. She'd slipped her hand into Harry's and to Jack's astonishment Harry didn't tug away. This was a child who'd hardly let himself be touched since his parents had died. 'We can have fun ourselves.'

'I'd like to come,' he said, thinking he did not want to be excluded from the fun his nephew could have with this woman.

Fun? He thought of the story she'd told him last night, of the pain she'd gone through, and he thought, here she was, dispensing fun.

'Then you need to know the rules,' Kate told him. 'Harry and I were discussing them while you dawdled.'

'I did not dawdle.' Astonishingly, she was laughing at him.

'You did so dawdle, didn't he, Harry?' She chuckled. 'But for the slowcoaches, here are the rules again. The main one is no touching.'

No touching? He'd been expecting touchy-feely stuff. Riding the dolphins? Maybe not, but close.

'Dolphins don't like being touched except on their terms,' she told him. 'All the dolphins in this pool were born wild. They're here because they've been injured, or orphaned, or somehow left so they can't survive in the open sea. But that doesn't mean they're pets. Some of them will nudge us. Hobble, for one, is a very pushy dolphin, but it's for him to decide, not us. But they do like playing. In the wild, dolphins surf. They seem to leap just for the joy of leaping when they're wild and free. But what's happened to them in the past means that they can't be free. Even though this pool is half the bay wide, it's not enough. They get bored so it's up to us to make them happy.'

And as she said it she walked into the water, lifted a beach ball floating in the shallows and tossed it far out.

It never hit the water. As it reached the peak of its arc a silver bullet streaked up from the surface. The dolphin's nose hit the ball square on, it rebounded, another silver bullet flashed from nowhere, the ball rebounded again— and landed in the shallows in front of Kate.

Harry had been standing behind Kate, open-mouthed with awe. Kate took a step back to stand beside him.

'This is our favourite game,' she said idly, and Jack

couldn't tell whether she was talking to him, to Harry or to the dolphins. 'But it makes me tired.' She lifted the ball again and threw, with exactly the same results. 'My arm aches,' she said. 'I've been tossing it for ages. That might be all I can do today.'

'I will throw the ball,' Harry said.

'You'd have to throw it far out,' Kate said dubiously, looking out to where one of the dolphins was rearing out of the water as if checking to see if the ball was returning.

'I can.'

'If you think so,' Kate said, and stepped back still further.

She didn't pick up the ball for him, though. The ball was floating about six feet in front of the little boy, in the shallows. He'd have to wade forward.

For three months Harry had been totally passive. He'd done exactly what he was told. He'd submitted to everything with stoic indifference. His world had been shattered and he'd been totally, absolutely joyless.

Now, as the world seemed to hold its breath, something changed. The little boy's shoulders, for months slumped and defeated, seemed to square.

He looked out at the dolphins and as if on cue they both reared, skating backwards. *Come on*, their body language said. *What are you waiting for?*

And then they dived, so deep they disappeared, and that message was obvious, too. Time to start the game now.

And while Jack watched in awe, and Kate said nothing at all, Harry strode purposefully out into the waves, grabbed the ball and tossed it high out over the sea to the waiting dolphins.

There was nothing for Jack and Kate to do but stand and watch. The dolphins did the rest.

This must be a game they played over and over with

withdrawn children, Jack thought. Harry was putty in their...flippers?

Harry threw the ball and they tossed it back to him, but as they did they gradually returned the ball a little further out. The waves were tiny and non-threatening. Harry found himself chest deep in the water before he knew it, but he was focussed only on the ball.

The next time he threw it, the dolphins flipped it back, but this time they flipped it over his head. He turned to grab it but before he could, a silver streak flew through the shallows, reached the ball before he did and flipped it back to where it had been landing before.

Harry lunged for it but the second dolphin reached it first, tossing it high again.

'It's mine,' Harry yelled, and grabbed for it, got it and tossed it out again. 'I got it, I got it,' he yelled, and he turned to Jack and Kate, his face alive with excitement. 'They tried to take it away from me but I got it.'

'Watch out, they're coming back,' Kate said, chuckling. 'They're champions at playing keepings off.'

The ball came back again and Harry pounced.

He was twisting on his injured leg, Jack realised. It had been badly broken. It still hurt to weight-bear so he usually tried not to use it. But Jack hadn't needed the physio's explanation to know where the problem lay—they all knew it. The only way Harry could get back the use of his leg was to use it.

He was using it now. It must be hurting, at least a little, but he was too entranced to notice.

'I can't believe this,' he murmured to Kate, while Harry was ball-chasing, out of earshot.

'It's our specialty,' she said, flashing him a look that was almost smug. 'None of your hospital physiotherapists have this—the means to make kids forget every single thing that's wrong with them. It's why this place is magic.'

'I don't believe in magic.' But maybe he did, he thought as he watched Harry pounce again. He thought of Susie, withdrawing into herself, desperately unhappy but still aching to play with the dolphins. He thought of Toby, his last days made happy. And he watched Harry.

It seemed like a miracle. Maybe he was even prepared to give magic a shot if it'd get Harry well again.

He was feeling disoriented, watching his nephew throw the ball, standing beside this woman in her crazy blue swimsuit.

He felt totally out of his depth.

Medicine. When all else was confusion, focus on medicine. It was a mantra that had served him well for years and he retreated to it now.

'His leg shouldn't be taking so long to heal,' he told Kate, trying to sound professional, two medical colleagues discussing a patient. Two medics in swimsuits. 'His femur was badly fractured but, even so, most kids with intramedullary nails are weight-bearing almost straight away. But we haven't been able to get him to use it.'

'He's had no reason to use it,' Kate said gently. 'It hurts and he's had enough hurting, losing his parents. Why put himself through more?'

He thought of the last physiotherapist Harry had seen—a young man not long out of training. He'd sat back and exclaimed in exasperation, 'Harry, you're not trying. I can't help you if you don't try.'

Harry's quadriceps were growing more and more wasted the less he used them, but that sort of reasoning got nowhere with him. Why should he try? It hurt and there was no point.

But now this woman had nailed it. She knew instinctively why Harry was like he was. They were in her hands, he thought, and his doubts were fading. Hers were competent hands. She knew what she was doing. He watched her subtly manoeuvre Harry, using the dolphins and the ball to have him bounce up and down, twist left and right. He threw and threw and the dolphins seemed to love every moment of it. Occasionally Harry winced and grimaced but he wasn't complaining. The dolphins—and Kate—seemed indeed to be magic. This was better than any medical intervention Jack could have thought of.

He'd love this back in Sydney. He thought of so many of his terminal cancer patients. How much joy this could give to families in distress.

He was willing to bet, even without his conversation, Kate would have got Susie back dancing.

He and Harry were blessed to have found this place.

Whoever Kate was, he thought, she was okay by him.

Finally Kate glanced at her watch and called a halt.

'It's almost lunchtime,' she told them. 'The dolphins need a break, even if we don't. Harry, later today you could do some leg exercises with Dianne in the swimming pool. She'll show you how to use a kick board so you can chase balls further. Then you can come back into the dolphin pool and see what the dolphins think of your new skills. Meanwhile, you can dig with Maisie or build sandcastles or have a nap or whatever you and Jack want to do. But now we're having hot dogs for lunch. Coming?' And she held out her hand.

Once again Jack found himself holding his breath. There was so much in those few short statements. *You could do some leg exercises in the swimming pool...* Using a kick board would be the best possible therapy for Harry—it would mean strengthening the quadriceps in the most natural way possible. The physios in Sydney had tried to get Harry to use one in the hospital therapy pool and Harry had refused, but here it had come out naturally, as if there could be no possible objection. Kate had moved straight onto hot dogs, and now she was holding out her hand as if she expected Harry to take it.

How did she do it? It wasn't only dolphins, Jack thought. This woman created an aura of absolute trust. If he was Harry he'd put his hand in hers, he thought, and he wasn't in the least bit surprised when Harry did.

'I like hot dogs,' Harry said in satisfaction, and then turned to look out to sea.

'Bye, dolphins.'

'Bye, dolphins,' Jack repeated, and then added under his breath, 'And thanks.'

They ate in the friendly dining-cum-lounge room. This was no aseptic hospital cafeteria but a homey area with a couple of bustling, smiley women ladling food on the tables. Each of the small dining tables was set with home-like tableware and place mats made by kids before them. Windows overlooked the bay, toys were scattered on the veranda, and through the arch, big comfy lounge suites and a massive billiard table made you think it was worth hurrying lunch because the world was waiting.

Susie was there, with her mum. The mum smiled and waved as they entered, and even Susie gave a cautious, teenager-not-wanting-be-noticed half-smile. Jack wasn't tempted to join them. Act as if nothing has happened, Susie's half-smile said, and that was fine by him. They found a place by the window and settled in.

Harry had retreated into his customary silence but he sat calmly by Jack's side and ate his hot dog without prodding. And why wouldn't he? Jack thought, heading back to the serving table for his third. He hadn't even been throwing the ball and he was ravenous—as well as exhausted. How had tension made him so tired?

'They tell you that you're bringing the kids here to make them well,' a burly guy sitting opposite said. 'What they don't tell you is that you end up doing as much or more than the kids.'

'It wasn't me doing the exercises,' Jack said, but the guy nodded toward the next table where a boy of about twelve was seated in a wheelchair, discussing the merits of which dolphin was fastest with a girl who looked like she'd been through chemotherapy.

'It takes it out of you just watching,' he said. 'I reckon every step our Sam takes, we take six. Your heart's in your mouth all the time. Wendy, the kid he's talking to…she's got some cancer called neuroblastoma and it's spread too far to fix. She's eleven, can you imagine what her folks are going through? But I saw her in the pool today, mucking round like she was just a normal kid and a happy one at that. Her folks were even laughing. Geez, we're pleased we found this place. Have another hot dog, mate.'

Jack did, and so did Harry. Then they retired to their bungalow for Kate's prescribed nap.

There was no protest from Harry. He was simply following rules and Jack thought, for a little boy whose world had been turned upside down, rules were good.

Harry slept. Jack did some highly satisfactory research on ballet dancers—it looked like he wouldn't be buried in sand after all—and then dozed.

Or sort of dozed. Images kept flitting through his mind.

Kate.

In less than a day he'd stopped thinking of her as Cathy. In less than a day he'd started thinking of her in a whole new way from how he'd considered her when she'd been his friend and lab partner back at university.

She was gorgeous.

She was hiding. The sensations of the morning faded and he was left with that one main thought.

She had to hide.

Jack Kincaid was a man who didn't do anger. Sure, there were things that annoyed him, but until Beth's death life had been pretty much how he'd anticipated. He'd had a great job, good friends, a beautiful girlfriend. He'd always known he was lucky. He'd appreciated his good luck, and he'd been making the most of it. In his work he'd seen how life knocked some people around but he'd never been knocked. What had he had to be angry about?

When Beth had died he'd been gutted. His perfect world had been knocked sideways but even then he hadn't been angry. Anger would have been better, he thought. Easier. Instead, he'd just felt empty.

Going back to work, taking his place in his perfect life again, that emptiness had remained. It was like there had been a gaping hole where his sister had been, where Harry's family had fitted.

And now, suddenly, for the first time, he felt anger, and it wasn't on behalf of his small nephew. It was for a kid called Cathy who'd been hauled from the life she loved and turned into the hunted. She hadn't needed to tell him how hard it must have been to run to New Zealand, to try and survive through a new university course, to cut herself off from every person she'd known in her past life. He could see it in the life lines on her face, in the shadows, in the way the laughter in her voice was edged with constant wariness.

This Simon had a lot to answer for, and Jack found himself staring out to sea and wishing he could face the bastard. Just once.

For Kate.

How corny was that? It was a caveman reaction, a testosterone-driven male protecting his own.

His own? Where had that come from? Kate was Harry's treating doctor—or treating physiotherapist and counsellor. He was here as Harry's guardian. There were professional boundaries that couldn't be crossed.

So why was he thinking of crossing them? He must have had too much sun, he decided, and on impulse he called Annalise.

'Jack!' Her voice was warm, but he could hear an edge of briskness, noises in the background that told him she was busy.

It was the weekend. She shouldn't be at work, but Annalise was often at work when she wasn't on duty. They both were. If you wanted to climb the career ladder, that's what you did.

'How's it going?' she asked. 'Dolphins, prayer flags and a bit of ear candling on the side?'

They'd laughed about this, both of them having the same reaction to alternate therapies. He was taking Harry here because Helen had insisted. He didn't believe in it.

But now, looking out over the bay, remembering the way Kate had stood back while Harry had turned again into a laughing, crowing little boy, thinking of Toby and of Susie, he thought he might well have been stupidly biased.

'It's early days yet,' he said cautiously. 'But I may have been wrong.'

'You're joking,' Annalise said. 'Are the dolphin mantras getting to you?'

'They're making Harry smile. I'm not asking for anything more right now.'

'Well, that's wonderful,' Annalise said briskly. 'If they can bring him out of his shell enough so he can come home and undertake real therapy then I'll even concede the uses of a little mantra-chanting. You're being mar-vellous, darling. Is there anything else? I really am busy.'

'Of course you are,' he said, and disconnected a mo-ment later feeling strangely dissatisfied. Why? She'd said what they'd both been thinking. And brisk phone calls when they were working was what he was used to.

He hesitated and then phoned Helen. Any emotion he'd missed with Annalise was more than made up for by his Harry's paternal aunt.

He told her about the dolphins and she sobbed.

'Oh, Jack, that's wonderful. He laughed? He spoke? Tell me again what he said.' She wanted to know every detail and by the end of the call he found himself think-ing maybe Harry should end up back with Helen. Five kids or not, there was no doubt Helen cared.

He'd argued hard with Helen to take over Harry's care. With memories of his quiet sister Beth, who'd spent her life engrossed in her karate and her science, happy with her boffin husband in her own little world, he'd seen Harry swamped by a world full of Helen's kids. But what sort of life could he give him as an alternative?

The question was too hard. Take one step at a time, he told himself.

'And I've been doing a bit of enquiring about Cathy Heineman,' Helen was saying, and her words pulled him back to the here and now like nothing else could. 'No one's heard of her for years. Everyone's astounded she's turned up there.'

Uh-oh. He'd forgotten he'd asked Helen about Kate.

'There's no need to make further enquiries,' he said, trying to sound as if it didn't much matter. And then he thought, Dammit, this was important, say it like it was. 'Helen, I talked to Kate—to Cathy—last night about the identity thing. It seems she's run from a violent marriage. She's changed her name. She doesn't want anyone to know.'

There was a moment's silence and then indignation. 'You could have told me that yesterday.'

'I didn't know yesterday.'

'Well, I hope I haven't blown her cover,' she said dubiously. 'I doubt it, though. How long ago was she married?'

'Several years.'

'There you go, then,' she said, relaxing. 'Old history. But I understand women who've faced abuse can't put it behind them. I don't think anyone I talked to yesterday would have taken it further. Most could hardly remember her, and no one seemed to know her husband.'

If you put Helen on a project she was like a terrier with a bone. How many people had she talked to?

'I wouldn't tell her I've been asking,' Helen said. 'You'll only make her fearful again, poor girl. And if she's helping Harry…from a selfish point of view I want all her attention on him. You keep them both safe, Jack Kincaid, and stay in touch. Give Harry a big kiss from me and tell him to get well fast.'

She disconnected, satisfied. Jack sat back and tried to feel satisfied as well.

He wasn't. He was disturbed.

Should he tell Kate that he might have blown her cover?

He thought of her smile, the way she'd laughed with Harry, her joy when her dolphins made Harry happy.

He'd be messing with that joy if he told her.

But if he didn't warn her…

He didn't have a choice, he decided. He had to. At least for the next couple of weeks he'd be here and could keep her safe.

Ha! That was the caveman in him. Neanderthal man, complete with club, protecting his woman.

But he looked out at the calm waters, at the peace of the bay, and he wondered how there could ever be threats here. Helen was right, Kate's marriage was history. Her husband would have long moved on. Telling her there might be the sniff of a threat would mar her peace for nothing.

I do need to tell her before I leave, he told himself. But I'm sure she's safe. Stop worrying. For now Helen's right. Let's just focus on Harry.

CHAPTER FIVE

LET'S JUST FOCUS on Harry.

That was all very well, Jack thought as the days wore on, but Kate was right there in his focus as well.

The more he saw her, the more entranced he became.

It wasn't that she was classically beautiful. Almost permanently dressed in a skin suit that flattered no one—a supermodel could hardly look good in skin-tight electric blue—with her often damp hair tugged back, her face devoid of make-up and her nose splodged with white zinc, she looked a world apart from the career-women in Jack's normal world.

Maybe that was the attraction—but surely the attraction was that she was so caring. The attraction was the way she made Harry smile—and the attraction was the way she smiled herself, her dimples, her freckles, her total and absolute focus on the child she was treating.

She loved her work, and she was good at it. Very good.

While Harry played with his dolphins he watched her discreetly manipulate play, so that Harry was forced to use his bad leg, so he was turning and twisting in a way he'd never do on land. The water took the weight from his legs so it wouldn't hurt as much, but still the unused muscles would be complaining. But because the dolphins were waiting for their new friend to join in with the next trick, Harry didn't notice.

In the normal physio sessions back at the hospital in Sydney, Harry hadn't tried. It had hurt and he'd wanted his mother. He'd been a ball of misery, and the more he'd curled into himself, the more the muscles had atrophied.

Here, under Kate's gentle guidance, he was stretching more than Jack had dared hope.

Kate couldn't be everywhere at once—she had a dozen small clients to treat—but the swimming pool physio sessions in the afternoon with the other trained staff were almost as effective. The physios back in Sydney had been good, Jack conceded, but they'd never had the enticement of 'If you can kick to the end of the pool, you and Hobble might be able to have a race tomorrow.'

'That's silly,' Harry had said, and once again Jack had caught his breath because this was Harry who was talking. Harry's tongue seemed to have atrophied as well, but now the muscles were tentatively in use again. 'I can't beat Hobble,' he said.

'He gets handicapped,' the physio told Harry.

'What's...what's handicapped?'

'We tell Hobble he has to zoom around the enclosure ten times while you use your board to kick from one side to the other. If he wins he gets a fish. If you win you get to feed all the dolphins a fish, so Hobble has to watch all his mates get one, too.'

Harry giggled, grabbed his foam kick board and started kicking. His wasted quadriceps meant he moved slowly but the up and down motion continued. With the dolphins used as a wonderful enticement to continue, Harry worked harder than Jack could believe was possible.

But as good as the support staff were, as successful as the physio programme was, it was Kate who did the most good. Harry and Kate had a one-on-one session each morning, supposedly playing with the dolphins, but there was a psychological component undercurrent running through it that stunned him.

The first time Harry 'beat' Hobble, Kate whooped with excitement. She fetched fish so Harry could solemnly feed all four dolphins. Harry giggled as Hobble took his fish and retreated to the far reaches of the pool—for all the world as if he was sulking at having to share. Kate chuckled, handed Harry the bucket of fish and said, oh, so casually: 'Oh, Harry, your mum and dad would be so proud of you.'

There was a moment's silence. The same sentence would have seen Harry shut down a week ago, but the dolphins were lined up for fish, Hobble was edging back and there was no corner to curl up in and withdraw.

Hobble sneaked in and knocked the bucket. A fish slipped out and Hobble had it. He reared back and Jack could have sworn he was laughing.

Harry smiled as well, but he still looked fearful. Kate had reminded him of things that were terrible.

'My mum and dad are dead,' he said.

And there was a breath-catcher, too. Harry had never referred to them, not once since the crash.

'That's right. They were killed in the accident where you broke your leg,' Kate said matter-of-factly. She took a fish and held it up. 'But I bet they're still proud of you. Some very wise people think that when parents die, part of them stays around for their kids. Not like they were, of course, but in the only way they can manage. It might be like the wind; when you feel a warm wind on your nose it's like a cuddle from your mum. Or the sunbeams. They could be your mum and dad smiling.

'Hobble, this is Splash's,' she said to Hobble, who was eyeing the fish she was holding, obviously wondering if another swoop would pay off. 'If you want to be the only one who eats fish then you have to beat Harry, and

Harry's getting faster.' She tossed the fish to Splash and watched the dynamics as the two fishless dolphins shoved their way to the front. Jack thought she was abandoning the deep and meaningful—but no.

'But I'm guessing the accident must have been really frightening, Harry,' she said.

All attention was on the dolphins. When the psychologists had talked to Harry at the hospital all the attention had been on him and he'd refused to answer.

This time he answered. 'Yes,' said Harry.

'Was Jack there when you woke up at the hospital?'

'Yes. And my Aunty Helen. But I want my mum and dad.'

'I'd want my mum and dad, too,' Kate said, again matter-of-factly. 'More than anything in the world.'

'I want them to come and get me. Now.'

They didn't have pockets in these damned suits. What Jack needed right now was a man-sized handkerchief. Or six.

'What are you worried about most?' Kate probed gently, handing Harry a fish. 'Don't let Hobble or Splash get this one.'

That took concentration. Harry might forget the question, Jack thought, but it was a huge question and Harry didn't forget.

'I don't think Mum and Dad will come back,' Harry said at last, in a dreary little voice. 'They're dead.'

'Don't forget the sunbeams,' Kate said, and Harry looked up towards the sun and let his nose warm up a little.

'No,' he whispered, and Jack wanted a handkerchief again.

'So who do you think should care for you, now that your mum and dad can't look after you?'

There was a long silence. Harry took a couple of steps

forward, gripped his fish, waited until the right dolphin edged close—and then put the fish in the waiting mouth just as Hobble swept forward to intercept.

Hobble missed out and Harry managed a quavery smile. The edge of the awful question had been taken away.

But it lay unanswered. Kate gave him all the time in the world, and finally he went back to it.

'My Auntie Helen will keep me,' he said at last. 'She said to Uncle Doug, '"One more kid doesn't make any difference. We'll scarcely notice."'

Jack drew in his breath. He remembered that conversation. Harry had still been in hospital. They'd all thought he was asleep.

'So your Auntie Helen and your Uncle Doug want you to live with them.'

'Yes.'

'Jack says they've given you a neat bedroom,' Kate said. They'd fed the dolphins the big fish but she had whitebait in the bottom of the bucket, tiny fish which could be eked out to extend a conversation. 'Is all your stuff there?'

'Mum and Dad aren't there.' He threw a tiny fish, hard, and the dolphins played a nudging game to get it.

'Your mum and dad aren't in your bedroom?'

'No. They're dead.'

'I can see that makes you feel angry,' Kate said, a no-brainer as he was hurling individual whitebait with force.

'They've left me with Aunty Helen.'

'You're with Jack now,' Kate pointed out.

'He doesn't want me. I heard my mum say that Jack and Annalise don't have time for kids. He'll go back to work. I want my mum and dad.'

Whoa. So much information, so much emotion, where there'd been nothing. He opened his mouth to say something but Kate shot him a warning glance. Don't mess with this, her glance said, and he subsided.

'You know, there's a whole lot of stuff you need to sort out,' Kate said. 'There's a whole lot of stuff that Jack needs to sort out, too. Missing your mum and dad is the biggest thing. It must hurt and hurt and hurt. But Jack loved your mother very much. He's her brother. He must be missing her just as much as you are.'

'He's not,' Harry said. 'He's a grown-up.'

'Grown-ups cry,' Kate said. 'Only sometimes they do it on the inside where you can't see. Is it like that for you, Jack?'

'Yes.' There was nothing else to say to a question like that.

'I think you and Jack are hurting just as much as each other,' Kate said. 'But, Harry, you have a sore leg as well, which means you get more chocolate ice cream to-night than Jack. Uh-oh. We've run out of fish. Is it time to take a shower before lunch? I think it's fish and chips today.' She turned to the dolphins and waved her empty bucket. 'No more for you, guys, but we're having fish for lunch as well.'

And the session was over, just like that.

Jack was feeling winded. He turned to leave the water, but suddenly Harry was right by his side, and a small hand slid into his.

'Do you cry inside?' he asked.

'Yes, I do.'

Harry looked at him quietly and then nodded.

'I want some fish and chips.'

Why was she so...discombobulated by the sight of Jack? Why was he doing her head in?

He seemed to be everywhere and yet he was only doing the normal thing dads did with their kids. Playing on the sand. Splashing about in the shallows. Taking a little time out to do long laps of the pool while she played with Harry. That was the hardest—her attention had to be totally on Harry and it was, but there was a part of her allowing her peripheral vision to take in his long, lean body stroking lazily through the water.

He was struggling with Harry—she could see it—and that twisted her heart a bit, too. He wasn't Harry's dad but he was trying. Every time Harry fell over, literally or metaphorically, he was there to pick him up. The little boy was withdrawn, mostly unresponsive, but it didn't stop Jack from hugging him, laughing with him, teasing him, caring for him.

He was a high-flying, ambitious medic. He was taking two weeks to try and bond with Harry.

He was also helping with the other kids here, subtly but surely. The way he'd responded to Susie had been more than kind; it had been empathic and sensitive. Susie was already talking about dancing again. Jack had used the admin. equipment to print pictures of famous dancers and Susie had them pinned to her wall. Why that did her head in she didn't know, but somehow a chord was touched. And she loved what he was trying to do with Harry. She didn't quite understand how these two could manage at the end of their two weeks here but for now he was trying and she had to give the man credit.

She didn't, however, need to give the man attention. Unfortunately her hormones thought otherwise.

'It's just that they're out of practice,' she told herself crossly. 'Get over it. The man's here as a client and that's all. Remember it.'

It was hard to remember when he was on her doorstep. She was watching telly when she heard a tentative knock on her door. It was eight o'clock but she was never off duty here. She was the only doctor so in any medical emergency she was available.

This wasn't a medical emergency. Jack was on her front porch, looking worried.

'I know,' he said, as she answered the door. 'You're staff and I'm a client. I'm supposed to make an appointment to see you. But I couldn't go to sleep tonight without saying thank you.'

'What I do is my job,' she said gently.

He was wearing chinos, an open-necked, short-sleeved shirt and no shoes. How fast her clients became beach bums, she thought. The blue sun suits were practical but they were a great leveller. Clothes could be used as a defence and there were no defences here.

'I didn't want to bring him here,' he said, and she hesitated and then stepped out onto the veranda. It was a corny soap she'd been watching anyway. The fact that television soap characters had become a big part of her life was irrelevant.

'You thought we were a pack of crystal ball gazers.'

'Something like that. I was wrong. I just…needed to say it.'

'Thank you for admitting it.' She glanced back through the screen.

'I'm interrupting.'

'Of course you are. Natalie's ex-husband has been found in bed with Natalie's stepmother and Jake has just revealed a secret baby to his fiancée. Oh, and Brandon's been caught with his hand in the till to the tune of eight million dollars.'

He glanced through to the television and saw a hysterical blonde yelling at a guy in handcuffs. 'Um… Wow!'

'You think you have dramas,' she said, and grinned. 'I listen to personal dramas all day and watch soaps at night to get them into perspective.'

'Can I watch, too?' he asked, and it was so much what she hadn't expected to him to say that she took a step back.

'Sorry,' he said hastily. 'I didn't mean...'

But he did mean and she could see it. Most of the kids here came with two parents, or a parent and support person. Jack was here alone.

She knew the need for adult companionship more than most.

'Harry?' she asked, but she knew already that this man wouldn't leave his nephew alone.

'He's asleep,' he said. 'The Fords have their teenage daughter with them, as well as Jacob of the injured spine. Misty Ford's currently sitting in my living room, playing computer games, with instructions to call me the moment Harry wakes.'

'You're paying her?'

'Of course.' He smiled. 'She's bored out of her mind and thinks this is an excellent plan.'

'So if I sent you back now, she'd be miffed.'

'I can go for a walk on the beach instead.'

She looked at him, this big, gentle man who seemed totally out of his depth with the future he was facing. He was asking for help, too, she thought. She should refer him to a session tomorrow. She did try to keep her professional life separate from her private.

But Jack had been a friend way back. A friend. How many of those did she have?

'Come in,' she said, swinging the screen door wide again. 'Welcome to the world where everyone else's problems fade into insignificance.'

So they watched a soap and then another one. Passion, drama, deception, intrigue, rage, tears, sex, all encapsulated in an hour and a half of hot television. When the second show came to an end Kate flicked off the telly and Jack felt winded.

'Whew.'

'What did I tell you?' she said, and grinned. 'Your problems are puny.'

'So I see,' he said, and smiled back, and she thought... she thought...

Um, that sort of thinking wasn't appropriate. This man was her client's uncle. Long ago he'd been a friend but surely now all her thinking should be on a professional basis.

But he was sprawled back on her settee. She'd provided him with a beer. He looked relaxed and a bit sunburned—she insisted on sun suits for the dolphins' sake but there was no way she could force people to keep applying zinc to their faces. He looked big and male and... gorgeous.

This man had been irresistible at uni, she thought. The women had come running. She'd watched from the sidelines and understood why.

Now this man was sprawled in her living room. Asking for help?

He'd come to thank her. That was fine, but if there was one thing she was good at it was reading undercurrents. The soapies had given him time out. He looked less strained than when he'd arrived, but there were still lines around his eyes that spoke of sleepless nights.

She had a sudden, irrational urge to reach out and smooth...

Um, no. She'd invited him in, given him a beer and let him watch soaps on her television. To take this further would be crazy. He didn't want it, and neither did she. He had a girlfriend, after all; and she did not do relationships. One Simon in her life was enough for anyone.

'Want to tell me about it?' she asked.

He met her gaze head on. This was an honest man, she thought suddenly. She could trust this man.

'I may have blown your cover,' he said, and, bang, there went her trust.

'Like…how?'

'I hope I haven't,' he said seriously. 'But when I first arrived, before I talked to you, I rang Helen about the discrepancies in your name. She did a bit of enquiring.'

'Oh,' she said in a small voice.

'I doubt it'll come to anything. It was simply a query as to what had happened to Cathy Heineman. I doubt any of the people she queried would have passed it on. Besides, your ex-husband would hardly be still trying to find you. Surely after all these years…'

'It'll be okay,' she said. 'Don't worry.'

But a shadow had flitted over her face as he'd said it. There was still fear. He felt like kicking himself. He shouldn't have told her. After all these years her fears must surely be unfounded but, still, he'd have done anything to stop that shadow of uncertainty.

'Cathy, I'm sorry.'

'It's Kate,' she said. 'But enough of the sorries. You did nothing I wouldn't have done in similar circumstances. Your first concern was Harry, and that's how it has to be. My private life is none of your concern. I only told you because…'

'Because once you were my friend?'

'Yes,' she said.

'I hope I still am.'

'Of course.' But something had changed, some indefinable thing. She looked totally vulnerable, he thought. She was wearing faded jeans and a sloppy windcheater, her curls were free, she'd been sighing and laughing over a soppy soap…and he'd scared her.

He wanted to tell her it was fine. He wanted to pull

her into his arms and tell her he'd protect her, no matter what it took.

What sort of Neanderthal instinct was that? She'd kick him out. What he was feeling was not appropriate. Not!

He was here to talk about Harry and apologise for the chink he'd made in her defences. That's what he'd come to her for. He'd thought he'd talk to her for a few moments on the veranda, sort out the tangle his thoughts were in and then leave.

So even though the conversation had been delayed for a couple of hours, even though there was now this irrational emotion zinging around the room, he needed to say what he'd come for. He needed to tell her his decision.

'I need to prepare Harry to live with his Aunt Helen,' he said, and he wasn't prepared for the silence that followed.

She was professional. This should be a professional acceptance. Relative telling doctor the patient's future living arrangements.

'Because?' she asked at last.

'Because Helen loves him.'

'So do you.'

'Yes, but Helen has a warm, loving home environment. It might be a muddle but it's a loving muddle. He'll feel safe there.'

'He doesn't feel safe there now.'

'He doesn't feel safe anywhere, but he'll grow accustomed to it.'

'He loves you. I watch the way he is with you. He trusts you.'

'He trusts his Aunt Helen.'

'Who has five children of her own. Whereas you...'

'I don't have any.'

'You don't want any?'

'I don't have a family.

'You have a girlfriend.'

'I do, but Annalise and I aren't parents.'

'You don't want to be parents?'

He sighed and raked his hair. Did he want to be a parent? He'd vaguely thought he would, but at some undefined time in the future. Not now. Not yet.

When Harry had been so appallingly orphaned, his own world had turned upside down. He'd spent every spare moment with his nephew. He'd seen how unhappy Harry had been with Helen's brood. His reaction had been to take him himself, accepting the parenting role.

Somehow, though, these past few days had him looking past immediate need. Cathy…Kate…had shown him that Harry could be happy again, and the little boy's whole life stretched before him.

A life with a career-driven uncle?

'If you could make him happy enough to settle into Helen's brood…' he ventured.

'That'd let you off the hook. You could go back to being uncle on the side.'

'I did think I needed to keep him with me,' he said. 'But if he can be happy…'

'Jack, I can't perform miracles. He's a loner, as is, I suspect, his Uncle Jack. No matter how good my psychology is, I can't turn him into something he wasn't before the accident.'

'I can't look after him.'

'You mean you won't.'

'If I must, I will. Of course I will.'

'But not with your girlfriend,' she said, suddenly softening. Suddenly seeing what the problem was. 'Not with Annalise.'

'She won't.'

'This isn't my problem, Jack,' she said softly. 'I'm sorry but you alone need to work this out. You can send him back to his Aunt Helen—of course you can—even though we both know that's not what's best for him.' She hesitated. 'But, Jack, kids can survive what's not best for them. They're tougher and more resilient than you think. He'll work out strategies for making the space he needs. There are all sorts of people in this equation—Harry, you, Annalise, Helen, Helen's husband and kids, all the complex interactions that go into making a family. Harry's needs can't necessarily take precedence over everyone else's. You need to work on finding a solution that's best for everyone.'

Was that what he wanted to hear? That Harry would learn to compromise and survive? He thought of the lone little boy and things twisted. To have him so badly hurt, and then ask more of him...

But the alternative? A hard knot of grief was tightening inside his gut, giving him nowhere to go.

'It'd be easier not to have a family at all.' His words were an explosion, fury at the situation in which he found himself, grief at the loss of the sister he'd loved, and helplessness at Harry's ongoing loss. His words came out as a mess of tangled emotion.

Kate winced, then reached out and took his hands.

'No,' she said. 'Never that.'

And he felt a sweep of shame. This woman had no one. She'd walked—no, run—from her world. She was frightened of a bully of an ex-husband. She was giving her all to her little patients, but for herself she lived in a world of medicine and night-time television.

That he should whinge about too much family...

'Wow, Kate, I'm sorry...'

'Don't be sorry,' she told him. 'You don't have to be sorry with me.'

'Because I'm a client?'

'Something like that,' she admitted.

'No,' he said, strongly now, recovering sense. As well as his anger and frustration, he now felt like a king-sized rat. 'I don't feel in the least like a client. I believe I'm a friend. Kate, I've loaded too much on you tonight and I'm sorry. It won't happen again.'

'It's what I'm here for.'

'To be loaded? Who cares for the carer?'

'I'm fine.'

'With your dolphins and your soaps? I don't think you are.'

'Jack…'

'I'm here for you,' he said, suddenly and strongly. 'I won't let that bastard come near you.'

'You can't stop him.'

'He won't. It's old history.'

'Yes.' But he knew she didn't believe it. After all this time, he could still hear the fear. *What had that low-life done to her?*

'Kate?'

She didn't respond.

He still had her hands in his. He cared for this woman, he thought, and the sensation was a powerful one. She'd been his friend.

She was his friend.

More.

There were so many emotions in his head right now he didn't know what to do with them.

Kate was just here. She was his hold on reality, he thought. His hold…

The television has long been turned off. The night was totally still. There was only the soft wash of the breaking waves on the shore as a background to their breathing.

As a background to their emotion.

Things were changing around them. What? Jack didn't know. All he knew was that Kate's hands were in his.

She was looking up at him and she was breathtakingly lovely. She was vulnerable... He'd made her vulnerable.

The emotional turmoil was building, building.

He couldn't bear it.

He kissed her.

One minute she was standing in front of Jack Kincaid, feeling angry, feeling betrayed about her own situation, feeling frustrated because this man wasn't seeing his little nephew's needs. The next she was being kissed. Solidly kissed. Ruthlessly kissed.

And she was kissing right back.

Why?

She had no idea.

Every particle of sense was telling her this was crazy. She should propel this man—this client—from her apartment and go back to being professional.

But she was over being professional. For this moment, for here and now, there wasn't a particle of room for it.

There was only room for Jack.

He was holding her hands, not tugging her close, just holding. She could pull away at any time. He wasn't pulling her into him.

He was simply kissing her. Their only connection was hands and mouth.

It was enough and more.

Warmth was flooding through her, and strength and need. The three emotions were warring and she had no space for anything else. Her mouth was under Jack's. He was kissing her almost as a question, but if it was a question, her whole body was answering.

The heat of this man. The strength. The sheer arrant masculinity.

She wasn't sure why she was being kissed. Anger?

Frustration? Need? It didn't matter. All that mattered was that she wanted him.

She should break away but, quite simply, she couldn't. She didn't want to and she didn't see the need to try.

How long since she had been this close to a man? Maybe never, her body thought. Simon had demanded her, had taken her, but had never asked.

This man was asking and the question was indescribably erotic, indescribably delicious.

Her hands tugged away from his as if they had a life of their own. They sifted through his thatch of gorgeous hair, tugging him closer, closer, closer.

She wanted him.

She felt the response of her body and her response amazed her. Stunned her. But it didn't frighten her. For whatever reason, however this had happened, it felt right.

Her body was responding to his need with an aching desire of her own.

Maybe she'd always wanted this man. Maybe... maybe...

Maybe this wasn't the time for thinking maybes. She was instinctively pressing close, moulding her breasts to his chest, her body responding with a need that was so primeval she had no hope of fighting it. She was kissing and kissing, and she wanted more.

She needed more.

Her hands flicked the buttons of his shirt and went underneath, feeling the hard, hot strength of him, the broad expanse of chest, the size, the strength...

Jack...

But he was catching her hands.

He was pulling away.

No!

And in the fraction of a second that took her to think

no, she regained her senses and so did he. He looked appalled.

He was appalled? To not be kissed for years and then have a man look at her as Jack was looking at her...

'That's the last time I ever watch soaps with you,' she managed, and heaven only knew how she managed it. She knew her voice was wobbling. Her whole insides seemed to be wobbling but somehow she said it and was inordinately proud that she'd managed it.

'Soaps must be...quite some aphrodisiac,' he said, and she was pleased that there was uncertainty in his voice, too. Though maybe not a wobble. This guy was testosterone on legs, and testosterone on legs did not wobble.

'Usually I watch them with Maisie,' she told him. 'Much safer. I...I think you should go home now.'

'Back to my bungalow.'

Did he think she'd meant back to Sydney? Did he think she'd meant he'd better leave the premises entirely because otherwise she might jump him?

'Back to your bungalow,' she agreed.

'Kate, I'm sorry.'

It needed only that. 'I'm not,' she snapped. 'It was a very nice kiss. Not quite so hot as Ronaldo on *Sunrise Babes* but, hey, a girl can only dream.'

He smiled, a tentative half-smile that did something to her insides that she didn't understand. And didn't trust.

'We should audition,' he said. 'Soaps R Us. Meanwhile, maybe we'd both best retreat to our own little worlds. It's much safer.'

'Much,' she said. 'Jack, from now on, consultations in my office, in work hours.'

'Of course.'

'Goodnight,' she said, and crossed to the door and tugged it open. Maisie was outside, sitting on the step. She looked vaguely astonished when she saw Jack inside. She walked forward, sniffed suspiciously and then climbed up on the settee where Jack had been sitting. Whatever child she'd been comforting tonight, clearly her job was done and she was coming home.

There were two seats in this sitting room. One for Kate. One for Maisie. No one else need apply.

'Goodnight,' Jack said, smiling at Maisie. He headed for the door, which Kate was holding open. He paused and touched her face, a feather touch with one strong finger.

'You're right, it was a very nice kiss,' he told her. 'We'd surely give Ronaldo a run for his money. But not wise. We both have a heap of sorting out to do.'

'Speak for yourself,' she managed. 'I'm sorted.'

'Then why do you still look frightened?'

'I didn't until you came along,' she said. 'Now maybe I have cause. Back off, Jack, and leave me in my secluded world.'

'I will keep you safe,' he said, and he saw her flinch.

'Don't say that,' she said. 'That's what Simon said from the time I was sixteen. My parents kept me safe and then Simon did, on his terms. My wounded dolphins are safe, but they're locked in a pen. They're so damaged they could never survive in the wild. Even though that pen's as big as we can make it, they're still locked in. Here…I didn't feel locked in until you arrived. I felt like one of the wild dolphins, free to come and go of my own accord. That's how I want to stay, Jack. Thank you for the kiss. It was lovely, but as for safe… I've depended on myself for that for a very long time, and I'm not about to relinquish control now.'

Why had he kissed her?

He hadn't been able not to. She'd been right in front of

him and every single part of him had wanted her. Every part of him had responded to her.

He'd felt this tug the first time he'd met her. She'd shrugged off his advances as unwanted but tonight she'd yielded. If he'd pushed... No, he wouldn't have needed to push. She had been his for the taking.

She was vulnerable. She was also his nephew's treating doctor, plus he was already committed. Semi-committed. More or less committed.

He didn't feel for Annalise what he felt for Kate.

But this was no ordinary situation. He was dependent on Kate to care for Harry, and somehow the professional side of him had surfaced. They needed to keep the doctor/patient relationship sacrosanct.

Except it wasn't. He'd gone to university with Kate. No court in the land would condemn...

Yes, but he'd condemn himself. That's why he'd managed to pull back. She was vulnerable, he needed her and the whole thing was unthinkable.

Except he was thinking. He was thinking so much his head hurt.

Thank God for babysitters. He needed a long walk. It was low tide, the moonlit beach beckoned and a man could walk for as long as he wanted. Until he found answers?

Were there any answers to be found? Who knew? All he could do was walk.

CHAPTER SIX

HARRY DID MORE healing in the next few days than he'd done in the three months since the accident.

Not just physically, Jack thought, although the physio-therapy sessions with the dolphins and in the pool were like gold. He was stretching his leg, he was moving his whole body, he was eating as if he'd been starved for three months—as indeed he almost had been because he'd lost all interest in food. In a week Jack could see a huge physical change.

The biggest difference, though, was in his mental well-being. He'd turned into a little boy again.

He had no worries here. This was a totally new envi-ronment and there was nothing to remind him of what he'd lost. He had Maisie, he had Kate and the rest of the awesome staff, and he had the dolphins. He tumbled out of bed every morning eager to see what the day would bring.

Eager to spend it with Jack.

Slight hiccup.

Had this been meant to turn into a bonding session between Jack and his nephew? Maybe it had. Jack had insisted on taking charge, even when it meant bringing him here. He might have realised it'd mean that every time something momentous happened, like when Wobble bounced the ball and Harry managed to catch it, or when

Kate released her hand under Harry's tummy and Harry managed to swim six whole strokes by himself without the kickboard, or when the bottom of the hole Harry and Maisie were digging high up on dry sand finally managed to ooze water, it was Jack he turned to.

Sometimes he'd give a tiny crow of delight. Most times he'd just catch Jack's gaze, make sure Jack was watching.

The same with Kate. She'd just catch his gaze, make sure he was watching.

Harry was bonding, hard and fast, with an uncle who wasn't sure where to take this.

Kate was judging that same uncle, waiting and watching to see where he'd take this.

It was up to him and it was overwhelming. Where was his nice, ordered world now?

Muddled.

Convoluted.

Tied up with Kate.

And there was another problem. The resort was small. Everywhere he went he seemed to see Kate. Her small patients adored her. Their parents thought she was awesome.

He thought she was awesome and the dilemma he found himself in kept growing larger.

She'd been his lab partner through medical school. He was starting to regret missed opportunities. Very much.

But he had a perfectly good relationship with Annalise. Didn't he?

No.

He'd always been on the outside, looking in, when it came to love. He never quite got it. He'd had relationships—of course he had—and they'd been fun and satisfying. But when Beth had come to him and told him she'd fallen head over heels in love, she'd glowed. His little sister had seemed transformed.

'It's hormones,' Annalise had said. 'That's all romantic love is, your body responding biologically to the need to procreate. Once that surge is over, that's when the trouble starts. You need to put it aside, go into relationships with your head and not your heart.'

He'd agreed, not necessarily because he knew she was right but because he'd never had that surge of pure, focussed desire—which was what he was having now, every time he passed Kate in her perfectly appalling blue skin suit.

Why? One kiss did not a relationship make.

Annalise would laugh and tell him to get over it.

'When are you coming home?' she asked at the end of the first week. 'I didn't think you'd stick it this long.'

'It's doing Harry more good than I dreamed it could.'

'That's great,' she said warmly. 'But Helen wants to help as well. Maybe you could come home and Helen could take over. If Helen's going to care for him long term, wouldn't that be sensible?'

Yes, it would.

'Jack, if I helped you dig another hole we might be able to tunnel under.' Harry's request was almost a whisper as he disconnected from the call. It was as if Harry was still expecting the world to slap him down. 'We might be able to join up.'

Joining... Fathering a seven-year-old.

He'd volunteered to do this. He'd pushed Helen into stepping back. He hadn't realised until now how big a deal it was—or how much he wanted it.

'Excellent,' he said, and started to dig. Maisie helped—sort of.

'You're becoming champion diggers.' Two feet down, and intent on their digging, Jack hauled his head from the hole and found blue-suited Kate smiling at them. 'If you go far enough, you'll reach China.'

'I don't want to go to China.' Harry pulled back and looked at her, anxious again. His anxiety was never far away. To say he was clinging was an understatement, yet when Jack thought of the silent waif of a week ago he was astounded at how far he'd come. 'I want to stay here.'

'This is a healing place,' Kate said, warmly but firmly. 'It's a place for you to get better. Most of the dolphins come here to heal, but when they're better they zoom off with their friends to where they belong. They come back to visit but they're free. It's the same for you.'

'Some dolphins stay,' Harry said stubbornly.

'Only the ones who are so badly wounded that they never get completely better, and that's sad. We all want to get better.'

'You stay here,' Harry said.

'Yes,' Kate said. 'Because it's my job to make people better so they can go home.'

'I don't have my home any more.'

Jack looked from Harry to Kate and back again. They were a pair, he thought suddenly. Two wounded creatures.

He couldn't do anything about Kate. Not yet. The *not yet* was an odd fragment of a thought, not fully formed. Maybe the *not yet* was a dumb notion that'd go away once the memory faded of an impulsive kiss.

But what came first, front and centre, was Harry staring bleakly up at Kate. Saying: *I don't have my home any more.*

It was time to make a stand.

'Yes, you do,' Jack said, and he reached out and hugged. Or tried to hug. The little boy froze as he normally did, but Jack kept his hold.

It's not only Harry making a decision, Jack thought. This is me. It's our future hanging on this moment.

He didn't have a clue what that future meant but somehow the last few days had changed things.

He loved this kid. This child was part of Beth.

He was part of him.

'We'll have a home,' he said, and still he held. 'To-gether.'

And finally, finally the child's body lost its rigidity. The tension seemed to seep out, slowly but surely. It was like a fight he'd been having for a very long time had suddenly been resolved.

'Will I live with you?' Harry whispered, in a voice that said he hardly dared to hope.

'Yes.'

'And with Annalise?'

'I don't know about Annalise.' He glanced up at Kate and she looked impassive. This decision was his, her body language said. It was nothing to do with her.

But somehow she'd made this moment possible. Some-how it had a whole lot to do with Kate.

She was beautiful, caring and...she was his friend.

Her body had fitted against his as if it was meant to be. He'd felt like he was coming home. The home he was offering to Harry?

That was a thought for the future, he told himself. What might or might not be between him and Kate was for sorting out when he and Harry had sorted themselves out.

'I don't know who else will live with us,' Jack said. 'But you and me, Harry...wherever we are, that's home.'

She had another client. Twelve-year-old Sam Harvey was waiting his turn in the dolphin pool. Another car accident victim, Sam had been more badly injured than Harry. He was paralysed from the waist down. He had three older brothers, all sports-crazed, and Sam couldn't see past the fact that he'd never be like his brothers.

His accident had been twelve months ago and he'd

pretty much retired into a morose, sullen world where his parents couldn't reach him.

The dolphins were reaching him. His brothers had been left at home. His parents were here, giving him their total support. He'd been able to swim before the accident and the dolphins were pushing him to swim harder.

None of his older brothers were anything more than competent swimmers. Kate had found videos of paralympians, swimming for gold. Sam was booked in for a month but in only half that time he'd gained self-confidence and he had a goal.

He had a family who'd see that goal through, no matter what it took. It felt great.

And now Harry had a family, too. Jack.

The thought was just good, she decided as she watched Sam swim. Sam no longer took all her attention. The dolphins were taking on her role as mentor. They were playing a weird version of water polo where the dolphins kept shooting the ball just out of his reach so he had to swim for it. If he was too slow they zoomed in and took it back.

His parents were cheering from the sidelines. Sam's swimming was growing stronger every moment. Kate was cheering, too, but a part of her was distracted.

A part of her had stayed up the beach, by a two–foot-deep hole, by a man who'd just decided to be part of a family.

He rang Annalise that night. She heard him out in silence, and the silence extended after he finished.

'You do realise that's the end of us as a couple,' she said at last, and he'd known it was coming. He'd expected it to hurt, but to his surprise it didn't. There was sadness, but no regret.

Once upon a time a professor in medical school had said to his class, 'Make the decision and say it out loud.

Then stand back and recognise how you feel. If it's the wrong decision your gut will tell you. Then be professional enough to change your mind.'

He wasn't changing his mind now.

He found himself thinking of Beth. She'd been studious, intent, totally committed to the work she loved. Her epilepsy had made her even more intent, finding an inner strength to achieve her goals. She'd had her work and her karate and she hadn't had time for boyfriends.

But at twenty two she'd reluctantly accompanied him to a student party. She'd met Arthur and she'd come home glowing.

Arthur had been a geek, a nerd, totally consumed with the need to discover new ways of keeping population water supplies unpolluted. That his shy sister had blossomed in this guy's presence had been unbelievable, but blossom she had. She'd adored him, and that flame had stayed bright until their untimely deaths.

But he didn't get it. He'd never felt like that, and there was regret but he felt no searing loss now knowing that what he and Annalise had had was over.

'I'm sorry.' There was nothing else to say.

'How will you manage your career?' She felt the same, he realised, and he wondered if she'd known it already. She'd never shared his concern for Harry; she'd made it clear from the start that it was his business.

'I don't know.'

'You'll need a bigger apartment.' She was masking disappointment with efficiency, and he was grateful. She'd been a friend for a long time and he didn't want to lose that friendship. 'I'll move back to mine at the weekend but you only have one spare room. You'll need a house with an en suite for a nanny. If you're coming back next week you should do some organisation now.'

'I'm not sure I'm coming back next week.'

'The Fraser International Symposium's the week after next,' she said, with horror. 'Jack, you're presenting. You need to be home for that.'

'I don't want to leave here yet. Harry's responding to treatment.'

'That's fantastic,' she said. 'But there are fine child psychologists here.'

'The dolphins are working.'

'You're kidding. Is this crystal-ball stuff rubbing off on you, too?'

'Of course it's not,' he said defensively, but he couldn't blame Annalise for her cynicism. He thought back to his scepticism of a week ago. How to explain?

'I've been trying to figure it out,' he told her, retreating into their common ground of medicine. 'I've done some reading. The thinking is that the dolphins somehow cause transfer of endorphins. Endorphins lift moods, ease tensions and therefore support receptive and learning abilities.'

'You're suggesting we buy every wounded kid a dolphin?' But she was caught. They'd had a good relationship, mostly based on their mutual passion for their careers. It eased what was happening now. She was open minded enough for her professional interest to be snagged.

'Not possible,' he said regretfully, thinking how amazing it'd be for Harry to have Hobble in his back-yard pool. 'Dolphins' brains seem as highly evolved as ours and they can't be held in captivity for our pleasure. Hobble, the dolphin Harry loves best, was caught in a net when he was young, cutting off the blood supply to his tail and leaving him permanently lopsided. He also lost his mother before he learned survival skills. Being here is the only way he can survive, but it's given Harry an enormous gift. It's a gift I can't bring home.'

'So you're risking your career, plus ditching a perfectly good girlfriend—'

'Anna...'

'It's okay,' she said briskly. 'I've never seen you as a dolphin-loving daddy, and if I missed that then who knows what other levels of incompatibility we have? But I'm still fond of you, Jack, and I'm worried. This is your career.'

'But it's Harry's life.'

He was standing on the veranda of his bungalow. Out in the dolphin pool Kate was playing in the water with a kid called Sam. He'd been watching Sam's progress as well as Harry's. Kate was performing miracles with him, too.

Kate...

Break off with one woman, take up with another? What was he thinking?

'It's your life, too,' Annalise said sharply. 'Jack, be sensible. Think about it. If you change your mind...about us, I mean...'

'There'll always be Harry.'

'Then you're on your own,' she snapped, finally letting anger hold sway. She disconnected, and Jack gazed out over the water at Kate and thought about that bald sentence.

You're on your own.

Harry was inside, sleeping. Sam finished his session. His parents took him back up the beach and Wendy took his place. Wendy was eleven years old. She had neuroblastoma with metastases and she had only months to live.

Wendy greeted Kate with joy and Kate gave her a hug and swept her in large, splashy circles before the dolphins came to join them.

This place wasn't magic just because of the dolphins, Jack thought. There was this woman called Kate.

You're on your own.

He watched Kate some more. Things were changing inside him. What was it with these dolphins?

What was it with this woman?

You're on your own. He wasn't, he thought. He was here with a woman called Kate.

Theirs was a professional relationship. She was the doctor, he was the guardian of her patient.

He'd known her when they'd been students. They'd been friends before. Could he manage that again?

Friends.

He thought again of Beth, floating home after that long-ago party, blushing fiery red because of a boy called Arthur.

Why was he thinking of that blush now?

Why couldn't he stop watching a woman called Kate?

He worried her.

He messed with her equanimity.

'Everything was fine until he arrived,' she told Hobble. She was floating on her back in the dolphin pool. She spent almost all her time focussed on her small charges' needs, but at dusk, when kids and parents headed in for dinner, she floated on the water and let herself be still.

The dolphins didn't try to play with her. They never did. They seemed to sense that she had a need for healing almost as great as her small patients. Sometimes they swam in slow circles around her. Sometimes they simply let her be.

They were wounded, too. Each one of the dolphins in the enclosure had a backstory of tragedy. They put her own history into perspective.

Until Jack had arrived she'd thought she'd achieved peace. Why had he disturbed that peace?

Because he might have inadvertently told Simon where she was?

That was one reason but weirdly it was a minor one. The bigger one was the way he made her feel. He was an old friend, caring for his small nephew. A man faced with his life being turned upside down.

A man who had a gift of tuning in to troubled kids.

A man who just had to smile at her and who made her feel...

Like she was losing control again?

She would not lose control.

The only child of elderly parents, she'd been controlled since birth, not by aggression but by the power of too much loving.

She'd adored her parents but their pressure had been relentless. All their focus, all their adoration, had been on her. If she upset one, the other would gently blackmail her. 'You know your mother's not well.' Or...'You know your father has a weak heart...' And then, even more of a sledgehammer... 'It'd make us so happy and proud if you married Simon. We could die knowing you were safe.'

Safe. Ha! As a promise, it sucked.

Jack could keep her safe. He'd said so.

How could anyone keep anyone safe? By gentle or not-so-gentle control?

She wasn't making sense, she decided, but, then, when had emotions ever made sense? All she knew was that she'd had a lifetime of control and she wasn't going back. Jack Kincaid might make her knees turn to jelly, but that was no reason to forget resolutions forged by fire. He might want to keep her safe, but she'd learned to run and she'd continue to run. Or at least hold desire at bay.

Hold Jack at bay?

She was reading too much into a kiss, she thought. She was reading too much into how Jack looked at her.

But she knew she wasn't.

She'd organised a formal counselling session for Harry late that afternoon. Maisie was lying at Harry's feet, while, at Kate's request, Harry was drawing a picture of himself with Hobble.

Jack was leafing through a magazine, trying to fade into the background. At first he'd felt he shouldn't be at these sessions, but Kate had insisted.

'Harry's had enough of being alone. He needs to know that every problem he has he can share with you.'

Jack was no longer arguing. The change in his nephew was amazing.

Harry finished his picture of Hobble but he'd only used a tiny part of the page. To Jack's surprise, the little boy drew a careful box around his picture of himself and the dolphin, then, underneath, he drew a table, and two figures sitting at the table.

And underneath the table a dog.

'That's you and Jack,' Kate said, and it wasn't a question.

'Yes,' Harry said. 'And our dog.'

'You and Jack would like a dog?'

'Yes.'

'And that's a picture of you and Hobble.'

'On our wall,' Harry said. 'So we'll remember it for ever and for ever.'

Then he paused, looked at his picture and added a box beside the table.

'Would you like to tell me what that is?' Kate asked.

'It's my ant farm.'

'You have an ant farm?'

'Yes.'

Kate looked a query at Jack but Jack gave an imperceptible shake of his head. This was news to him.

'So this is your house, where you live with Jack.'

'Yes,' Harry said, and he cast Jack a look that was half scared, half defiant.

The moment had come. There was no backing out now.

'That's right,' Jack said. 'You'll need to paint a bigger picture of you and Hobble for our real wall.'

'Yes,' Harry said, still a bit defiant, still suspicious.

'But it won't be the house where you lived with your mum and dad,' Jack said, because it seemed important to say it like it had to be. 'I work at the hospital and your house is too far away. We'll need to find a house just for us, somewhere closer.'

There was a long moment while Harry thought this through. Jack could see the conflicting emotion on his small face. He saw anguish, loss—and finally bleak acceptance.

'Will we find a new house?' he asked in a small voice.

'Yes.' A kid and a dog…a hospital apartment was no longer feasible. 'You can help choose it.'

That made him brighten a little.

'With my own bedroom? And a window with a tree?'

Harder, but manageable. 'Yes.'

'Will Annalise live with us?'

'No. Just you and me.' He looked dubiously at the picture. 'And a dog and an ant farm, though it might take a while before we can find a dog.'

'Can we find one like Maisie?'

Oh, hell, why not? He had a sudden flash of dog-sitters and big back yards and his social life going down the toilet, but there wasn't a lot of choice. 'Yes.'

'Why won't Annalise live with us?'

'She doesn't like dogs.'

It was obviously the right answer. 'All right,' Harry

said, turning back to his picture. 'The dog can stay in my bedroom. And my ant farm.'

'Of course,' he said weakly, and Kate gave him an approving grin and went back to concentrating on Harry's picture.

Harry and Jack and Dog and ant farm?

Move over, Harry, he thought. I need counselling myself.

CHAPTER SEVEN

TELEVISION HAD FAILED her. This was a remote community, there were exactly three channels to choose from, and tonight, unless she wanted news of the day, hyenas feeding off dead zebras or a documentary about weight-loss programmes, she was lost.

Maisie was off doing her dog therapy with their latest patient arrival. Kate was on her own.

She wanted diversions but there weren't any. She couldn't stop thinking about Jack.

She'd listened to the commitments Jack had been making in the counselling session and she'd been astonishingly moved. He was losing his girlfriend, his apartment, his lifestyle.

Maybe he hadn't thought it through, but she'd watched his face as he'd said it and she knew that for now he believed in what he was promising.

Resolutions didn't always last. Don't believe in people, she told herself, almost fiercely. Once upon a time she'd believed in Simon.

Restless, she headed out to the beach. The tide was low, and the moon hung silver over the water. She could walk as far as she wanted.

She never went far. Like her injured dolphins, she wasn't leaving.

Why, tonight, was she suddenly thinking of leaving?

Because a man called Jack had her…discombobulated. For discombobulated she certainly was. She needed to get herself in order, she told herself. Her day started at dawn. She needed to head for bed.

To sleep? Not possible.

She had to try. She'd been walking for an hour and she needed to be up at dawn.

She walked slowly across the sand hills, past the bungalows holding sleeping children and their parents.

She walked past Jack's veranda, keeping to the shadows in case he was outside.

He was outside, on the phone.

She had no right to stop and listen but there was no way her feet would obey her conscience. She stopped and she listened.

'Helen, what's happened to his ant farm?'

He was sitting on the cane settee with a beer. Harry must be asleep, she thought, and Jack was on speakerphone. Why not? It'd be easier to sit back and talk while gazing out at the moon.

He must have just come out, Kate thought, or he'd have seen her on the beach. The path up to the bungalows was heavily planted, with side paths to the individual accommodation. That was lucky. She didn't want him to see her.

Why? She hardly knew, and she certainly had no right to eavesdrop. But what was between them was starting to feel strange; uncharted territory. She should slink off into the shadows, but somehow she was caught. What Jack was saying would impinge on Harry's life, she told herself. Maybe she even had a duty to listen.

Ha! Yet she stayed where she was, unashamedly eavesdropping.

'What are you talking about?' Helen was demanding.

'An ant farm. I gather it's important to him. It's a tank like a skinny goldfish bowl, full of ants. I used to have one when I was a kid. Did you take it to your place when we cleared up?'

'I can't remember seeing it. Hang on and I'll ask Doug.' There was a muffled conversation while Helen talked to someone in the background and when she came back on the line the news wasn't good. 'Doug says he wondered what that was. It was in Harry's room, a tank full of dirt. He binned it.'

Uh-oh. Kate had known Harry for little more than a week yet even she knew what was important.

This was important.

'Put Doug on,' Jack said, and she heard the tension in his voice. He must have also realised the enormity of this loss.

But Doug had a good memory. Jack pushed for details and Doug could describe size and shape.

'Right,' Jack said. 'I'll go on the internet and order a replacement. Can you set it up before we get home?'

'Where do I get ants?' It was Helen again, sounding horrified. 'Do you want us to go out to the garden and dig 'em up?'

'He'll know the difference between home ants and the ants he had,' Jack said. 'This is one kid you can't fool by swapping budgies.'

Kate smiled a little at that. How many kids had been spared trauma when their pet bird died by parents simply replacing them? But…ants?

'You're saying he can pick individual ants?' Doug demanded.

'He's his mother's son and I know my Beth,' Jack said simply, and then corrected himself bleakly. 'I knew my Beth. She'd know every characteristic of every ant. We may not be able to replace the exact ants but they'll be a certain breed. I'll grill him tomorrow and hopefully order them on the internet. I know we can't get it looking exactly the same but we can tell him the twins tipped it over and you've replaced the soil. His favourite ants might have got squashed. It's a compromise but it's the best we can do.'

'I don't believe this.' Helen came back on the phone. 'All this worry, and we're fretting about ants? And when are you coming home?'

'When the ant farm's ready.'

'So Harry's coming back here?'

'No,' Jack said, firmly and surely. 'Helen, your family is great. I know you and Doug love Harry to bits, but he's a kid who needs silence. He stays with me.'

'He'll get more than silence with you,' Helen snapped. 'He'll be totally isolated.'

'He won't be.'

'You work six days a week, twelve-hour days. What sort of life is that for a child?'

'I'll change things.'

'You need a wife. Annalise?'

'She's no longer in the picture and even if she was, I couldn't ask this of her. This is my call. Helen, I can organise my life. I can make things good for Harry. Trust me.'

'It's a child's life,' Helen said bleakly. 'It's a huge trust.'

'Don't I know it,' Jack said. 'I'll do what I have to do. Watch this space.'

He'd disconnected. Kate stood silent. She should back away, she thought. She had no right being here.

'You can come out now,' Jack said, and her world stilled.

There was nothing for it. She emerged from the shadows, feeling like a criminal.

'I'm sorry,' she said. 'I was coming up the path and didn't want to interrupt.'

'You want to help me choose ants?' he asked, as if she'd done nothing dishonourable at all.

'Jack, I didn't mean—'

'I knew you were there,' he said. 'Eavesdropping's only a crime when it's successful.'

'I had no right—'

'You have every right. You're transforming my nephew's life. You want to listen in on us twenty-four seven, it's fine by me. We need what you're doing, Kate. We need you.'

As a statement it took her breath away. Trust... He looked down at her and smiled, and if she'd had any more breath to spare she'd have lost it then.

That smile...

'Ants,' he said. 'Research. Glass of wine first or are you on call?'

'No wine,' she said, because with that smile she did not need alcohol.

'But you have time for ant-farming?' He shifted sideways on the settee and gestured to the laptop in front of him. 'Want to take a look? I know it's not *Sunrise Babes* but, hey, I bet what goes on in these closed, glass communities will make your eyes pop.'

And who could resist an invitation like that? She headed up the steps, still feeling shamefaced, but Jack had moved on.

'Gel?' He was staring at the screen. 'I thought you just used dirt. When did ants start needing gel? And it says you can't order queen ants on line. Quarantine between states? How did Harry get the first one? You're going to have to help me here, Kate. Tomorrow's counselling session has to be all about how he feels about his ant farm, and subtle questions as to technical detail on how he got the last one. And look at this! They shove the dead ones up the top and you're expected to remove them to prevent disease? They have to be kidding. Maybe that's why all mine died when I was a kid. I think I need counselling. I'm an oncologist, not an ant funeral director. I think I'm in trouble.'

And then he glanced at her again and his smile faded.

'Maybe we're both in trouble,' he said softly, and she met his look for a long moment—and then flinched and went back to looking at a screen full of ants.

CHAPTER EIGHT

THEY SPENT A ridiculous hour researching ant farms. 'I can put it on my CV now,' Kate said proudly at the end of it. 'Doctor, physiotherapist, counsellor, dolphin expert and now ant-farm advisor.'

'Is there no end to your skills?' Jack demanded, and she grinned.

'Nope.'

'Do you take an active hand in caring for the dolphins?' he asked.

'We all do,' she said simply. 'This place runs with a team of committed professionals, and every one of us can turn their hand to anything. Even Bob, the groundsman, is expected to interact with the kids, and he loves it. We don't have a full-time vet—that's a gap—but we get on-line help. Usually injured dolphins don't come straight to us. They're found in more populated areas so the initial vet work is done there. They're brought to us to give them time and space to heal. There's not a lot of hands-on work to do for a healing dolphin. Dolphin heal pretty magically anyway.'

'What do you mean?'

'I mean if a shark took a chunk from your backside you'd be remembering it for the rest of your life, but for some amazing reason dolphins regenerate torn flesh. They arrive looking gruesome, yet as soon as we get them non-stressed, their regenerative power takes over. This place has released hundreds of dolphins, slightly scarred but ready to fish another day.'

'To the local fishermen's displeasure.'

'There is that,' she admitted ruefully. 'But when the founders of this place set it up they chose a place well away from any fishing harbour. We do get locals complaining that we're ruining their sport. Someone even shot a dolphin last year, but he got such appalling local press that he's not been heard of since. Gotta love a dolphin.'

He smiled, feeling the pride she so obviously had in this work. And for a stupid moment he felt...jealous?

Jealous of this slip of a girl, burying herself at the edge of nowhere, passionate about her patients and her dolphins but nothing else.

He thought of the life he lived back in Sydney. He was in charge of a large, modern cancer centre, but it was part of a huge teaching hospital. He spent so much of his time fighting for funding, organising support for patient care, dealing with the requirements to hold a large medical team on focus, that his contact with patients was becoming less and less.

This might be so much more rewarding.

'It's not all it looks,' Kate said, and he glanced at her sharply. She could guess his thoughts? She'd done psychology, he thought. Dangerous. He should stop thinking immediately.

'I need to fight for my patients, too,' she said. 'Every one of them has special needs, and those needs often can't be held in abeyance while they're here. I have two kids who are still on chemotherapy. I have to fight to get the drugs, fight to be given the knowledge how to administer them. If your Harry had come here with cancer, I'd have done my homework before he came. I'd have been onto his doctors, and I'd have pleaded with them to give me the resources to keep him safe.'

'You didn't have those resources with Toby Linkler.'

'He'd run out of options,' she said bleakly. 'If he'd stayed in Melbourne, if the family had wanted it, he might have been given another round of chemo, but the medical team who looked after him knew it was the end.'

'So this is partly a hospice.'

'It isn't,' she said hotly. 'Toby and his mother came here to heal, and that's what they did.'

'He died.'

'Yes, he did, but he didn't spend his last few days dying. He died with the sun on his face and dolphins swimming around and not a ventilator or IV line in sight. Jack, if anyone thought a last round of chemo was anything more than a forlorn hope, I'd have fought tooth and nail to get it for him. I've refused kids who need ongoing treatment if their doctors won't agree to let me administer it. I can't take kids sometimes because I don't have the skills to treat them.'

'You need me here long term,' he said, joking, and she looked at him in the moonlight and there was no answering smile.

'You're here to be treated,' she said simply. 'And then I'll let you go.'

'Me? Treated?'

'You're figuring yourself out. For instance, the importance of one ant farm, for you and for Harry.'

'I would have worked that out back in Sydney.'

'You might not have if you hadn't taken this time out.'

'So what about you?' he asked. 'When do you consider yourself healed?'

'I am healed.'

'Says the woman who spends her nights watching soaps.'

'I'm happy here, Jack,' she said, but she knew it sounded defensive. She knew she didn't sound like she meant it.

But she did mean it. The work she was doing was important. She was making a difference to people's lives. What else could she ask for?

Release from fear? A release from the knowledge that she was still hiding?

Release to start again, with someone like...someone like...

'You're doing an amazing job,' Jack said gently. 'Will you do it for ever?'

'Why wouldn't I?'

'Would they have trouble finding a replacement?'

'What are you suggesting? That I walk away? Why would I want to?'

'You might get tired of *Sunrise Babes*.'

'How could anyone tire of *Sunset Babes*?' she demanded in mock indignation. 'We have a divorce, a sex scene and at least one catastrophe a week. That's much more exciting than real life.'

'Would you like to go back to real life?'

His tone was gentle, and suddenly she stopped fighting to keep barriers in place. He was a friend, she thought suddenly. He'd been a friend when she'd been a student. Why shouldn't she say it like it was?

'I've been hiding for so many years I've lost count,' she said simply. 'I don't know any other way. This place makes me feel safe as nowhere else does. I'm like Hobble with his malformed tail. This is my home.'

'You don't have a malformed anything,' he said, even more gently.

'But when I hear a car arriving, I still flinch,' she said. 'How stupid is that? When I was at university in New

Zealand every time I heard a door slam in the night I'd wake in terror. I'm worse than Hobble.'

'Just how badly did he treat you?'

She gazed at him for a long moment. She didn't talk about her relationship with Simon. Talking about him brought back the fear, brought back the terror. But Jack was asking. Jack was her friend.

She tugged up the sleeve of her shirt, rolling it to the shoulder, and held out her arm for him to see.

They'd done a great job repairing her elbow. All that was left was a long incision scar. The scar was neat. The scars from the cigarette burns were not so neat.

Jack stared down at the scars for a very long time. She didn't say anything. She didn't have to.

'This isn't the extent of it?' he said at last, and her silence was answer enough.

He swore. The oath was almost under his breath but its savagery was so intense it frightened her.

'Don't,' she said. 'Please... It's over.'

'It's not if you're still terrified.' He reached out and grasped her arm before she could pull the sleeve down. No. He didn't grasp, she thought. He simply held. This wasn't a man who grasped.

'It's not over while that bastard walks the planet,' he said, quite lightly but the venom underneath was frightening all by itself. 'Did he go to jail for this?'

'He went to jail for fraud.'

'So you never had him face justice for abuse?'

'I... There was no need.' How to say she'd have never had the courage?

'There's no statute of limitations on abuse charges,' he said. 'I imagine you received decent medical treatment?'

She nodded, remembering lone visits to emergency departments over the years, trying to choose hospitals where she knew no one. Young doctors with shocked faces. Counsellors who'd told her to go to the police, to break free.

But it would have been his word against hers in a criminal court, and she hadn't had the courage to face him down. If there'd been outsiders who'd witnessed the beatings, if she'd been sure the charges would stick and she wouldn't have to face him afterwards, then maybe. But it would have killed her parents to know this about the man they'd thought was wonderful, and if the charges hadn't been proved, what then? Only when he'd robbed her mother had the cycle finally been broken.

Jack's expression had grown even more grim. 'Then we can still nail him,' he was saying. 'Put him back in jail. Kate, you need to face this head on.'

'No!'

'Why not?'

'I don't want to face him ever again. He made me feel...worthless.'

'While you're running you're still a victim.'

'I'm not running. I'm safe.'

'With your dolphins and your soaps.'

'Jack, don't. Please...' She hesitated, trying to get rid of the feeling she had every time she thought of her ex-husband. He still made her cringe. He still made her feel as if she'd been a coward and a fool, and she didn't want to go there.

'What about you?' she asked, in a desperate attempt to deflect the conversation, and she saw Jack's brows hike.

'What do you mean, what about me?'

'What are you running from?'

'Nothing.'

'So you're a normal heterosexual male in his mid-thirties who just broke up with his current girlfriend with apparently barely a touch of emotion.'

'I'm a seething mess of conflicted emotion inside.'

She smiled at that, but she was watching his face and saw that maybe he wasn't joking. But this man wasn't carrying a broken heart.

'Even at uni,' she said thoughtfully, 'you went out with the most beautiful women, the most popular, the women who were self-contained. The women who'd never cling. I saw you go through at least half a dozen girlfriends during med school and I can't remember any of them who seemed like they needed you. Or you needed them. And here you are, breaking up with Annalise and hiding your mess of conflicted emotion extraordinarily well.'

'That's 'cos I'm a guy.' But he seemed uneasy. 'You know guys don't show emotion.'

'There were lots of couples formed during med school,' she said, still thoughtful. 'Friends to lovers. It made sense, we got to know each other so well, but looking back…did you and I get on so well as lab partners because we knew the boundaries? I had Simon stopping me from getting close to anyone. You had your humour and your intellect and you used them as a shield.'

'Is this your psychology training talking?'

'Maybe it is,' she said, striving to keep it light. But it seemed to her that strain was starting to appear around Jack's eyes. Her faint suspicion that he had his own ghosts was starting to crystallise into full-blown surety.

'So tell me about your mum and dad,' she said lightly. 'Were they a happy-ever-after story?'

'This is hardly appropriate.'

'It's not, is it?' she agreed. 'It's just that you now know all about me and I know nothing about you. Except I know your parents were wealthy. The other med students used to talk about your dad with awe. He was a QC, wasn't he? And you had a little sister called Beth who I know you adored. You want to fill in the gaps?'

'No.'

'Why not? Are you running from shadows, too?'
'No!'

She didn't talk back. She simply hiked her eyebrows in a mock mirror image of his own gesture, folded her hands, looked out to sea—and waited.

What was going on? One minute he was probing about her past, pushing her to do something, being proactive. He was playing the male role, the protector, acting as he would have if it'd been Beth in the role of the abused.

Suddenly she'd turned the tables.

She was no longer pushing. She was simply...waiting.

She was an extraordinarily restful woman, he thought, and then he reconsidered. No, she was just extraordinary.

But she was asking him to reveal personal stuff. He didn't do personal stuff.

Was that why it didn't hurt that Annalise had agreed to move from their apartment with minimal fuss? Was that why he always chose girlfriends who saw him as a useful accessory rather than the love of their life?

Did he see them the same way?

He'd barely thought about it until now. But maybe he had, he acknowledged. Maybe he'd thought about it and blocked it out.

He remembered how he'd felt when Beth had met her Arthur.

She'd come home glowing, she'd wafted round in a mist of happiness, and he remembered being...fearful. That she'd left herself exposed.

She'd married, Harry had arrived and for the first time then she'd revealed to him how frightening it was.

'If anything happened to them, I'd die,' she'd told Jack simply. 'Arthur and now Harry...I love them so much, they're my whole heart.'

'How can you do this?' he'd asked. It had been a rare

moment of truth between the siblings. Normally they'd avoided talking about their home life. 'How can you expose yourself to what Mum and Dad put up with?'

'Because it's worth the risk,' she'd said simply, and smiled down at her sleeping baby. 'Oh, Jack, I hope you find that out for yourself.'

And then Beth herself had died and every single one of his fears had crystallised. He'd stood at the graveside and felt empty. Dead himself. Annalise had stood beside him but he hadn't held her hand and she hadn't tried to take it. They'd respected each other's space.

Kate was still waiting. She was still watching the sea, giving him space. She was a woman who'd seen it all.

Why not tell her?

'My parents...overdid the love thing,' he said, keeping his voice neutral. After what Kate had been through, this was no big deal. Poor little rich boy? What was he on about?

'How can you overdo love?' Kate asked, and then hesitated. 'No, that's a dumb question. My parents manipulated me through love. Simon swore he loved me. Love has weird guises.'

'Theirs was passion,' he said, suddenly grim. 'They married in a storm of passion—a two-week courtship and then off to Gretna Green, for heaven's sake, because my mother thought that was the most romantic place on earth to be married. Only it rained and the hotel had lumpy mattresses so they fought at the top of their lungs, they broke up, and then they came together again and headed for another romantic "wedding" in the Seychelles. And that was the entire foundation of their marriage. My father was a lawyer at the top of his game. My mother was an interior designer, a good one. Both of them had enormous professional respect.

'Both of them used their marriage to rid themselves

of stress, to shout, to fight, to break up, to passionately come together again. Beth and I were the catalysts for a lot of the conflict. Our parents were either in a passionate clinch like hot young lovers, not able to keep their hands off each other, even in front of us, or they were hurling things at each other. Their fights were vicious and real, and Beth and I were in the middle.'

'Tough.'

'You said it,' he admitted grimly. 'I hated it. Beth was four years younger than me, she was epileptic, stress brought on attacks and I seemed to spend my childhood protecting her. Maybe I did too good a job. Maybe that's why she was able to fall so passionately in love with Arthur.'

'That marriage worked?'

'It seemed to,' he admitted. 'But it was a huge risk. Love leaves you wide open—and now she's dead.'

'Would she still be dead if she hadn't made the decision to love?'

He closed his eyes. 'I know. Her death was random. One drunk driver late at night, ice on the road... But she knew the risks. When Harry was born, she made me swear I'd look after him. As if she knew...'

'Every good parent thinks about worst-case scenarios,' she said simply. 'They talk it through, do the asking, then get on with their lives. But you...maybe love cost you your childhood, and here you are, losing again through love. Maybe you're the one who's scarred.'

'I'm not scarred.'

'I think you are,' she said gently. 'Almost as badly as Harry.'

'Kate—'

'Use this time,' she said urgently, rising. 'Jack, this is time out for both you and Harry. You have so much to think about. If you're uncomfortable talking to me,

then think about using Louise—she's a competent psychotherapist.'

'I don't need a psychotherapist!' It was an angry snap,
but Kate didn't flinch.

'This is a healing place,' she said softly. 'Yes, we do
have kids who come here when they're dying but even
in dying, the family can find a kind of peace. If you give
in to that peace, that acceptance, we can help you for the
rest of your life.'

'It's Harry who needs help.'

'Via you. Harry needs you. Are you prepared to open
yourself up to him? To anyone?'

'I've just organised his ant farm. How much more do
I need to do?'

'I think you know how much,' she said softly, and
then, as if she couldn't help herself, she raised her hand
and traced the contours of his cheekbones. 'You're a good
man, Jack Kincaid, but you do need help.'

'Says the woman in hiding.'

'Jack…'

He caught her hand in his, and he held. The night was
still between them. Underneath the veranda a tiny rock
wallaby was snuffling through the bushes. Trusting. Here
in this retreat, there was no threat.

So why did Jack suddenly feel that there was a threat?
Why did he feel exposed?

Because of what this woman had said?

Because of what this woman was?

But right now his emotions were changing. Needs
were changing. They'd been talking of the past, of things
that had threatened them both.

Right now was…now.

And right now he wanted to kiss her. It was as simple
as that. The conversation faded. Reservations faded. He
looked down into her face and he thought what a gift had

been in front of him all those years ago. He'd accepted her statement that she'd had a boyfriend. He hadn't explored past it.

Maybe he hadn't wanted to explore past it. Maybe he was running as scared as Kate was.

'"Physician, heal thyself"?' he said, striving for lightness—and failing. 'Maybe...it should read, "Physician, heal each other."'

'Jack...'

'Maybe we could try,' he said softly.

He kissed her then, a gentle, questioning kiss that he didn't understand. He'd kissed her before, with passion. Tonight passion had taken a back seat. This was a kiss of questions, an asking if things were possible, a kiss that asked where they could take things from here.

She kissed him back and he felt the same uncertainty in her. The same need?

The kiss went on for a very long time. They simply held, warmth flooding through, questions being asked and answered, a future tentatively opening before them. It felt right, he thought as he held her close and felt the sheer wonder of her. It felt like the beginning of something...amazing.

She felt right. She...fitted. It didn't make any kind of sense, but all he knew was that she was right for him.

But when they finally pulled apart, when finally the kiss ended, as all kisses eventually had to, she backed away in the moonlight and her look was troubled.

'What?' he said, and touched her lips with his finger. 'What, my love?'

'I'm not your love.'

'No, but—'

'Neither am I an answer to your problems.'

There was a moment's silence. The trouble deepened.

She was withdrawing, her armour slipping back. It was imaginary armour but he could almost see it.

'I don't know what you mean.' He reached to hold her again but she shook her head.

'No. Jack, I love…' She touched her lips. 'No, I mean I like you kissing me. I like you touching me. Our friendship goes back a long way and you know how isolated I've been. Maybe my reaction to you is a response to that isolation. Maybe it's not. But you and Annalise—'

'It's over.'

'That's right, it's over,' she said, sounding still more troubled. 'And isn't that the problem?'

'I don't know what you mean.'

'You must see it,' she said. She was struggling to sound calm, as if she was trying to figure things out as she said them. 'Jack, you have a child to care for. Your girlfriend's ditched you. You're facing a future as a lone parent and it scares you. And now you're kissing me.'

'This has nothing to do with—'

'I think it has.' She closed her eyes, and when she opened them she'd withdrawn still further. 'Jack, my parents needed me for physical care and their love for me was bound up with that. My dad was sixty when I was born and Mum was over forty. My birth almost killed Mum, and Dad already had heart problems. My needs came a poor second to their health, to their needs. My job was to make them feel secure, make them proud, not rock the boat. And then Simon came along and I fell in love with him but he needed me for my money. He needed me to play the subservient wife. Even when I was struggling to escape from Simon I was still trying to protect my parents. I don't know whether you can understand this, but I don't want to be…needed…again.'

'Kate, I would never…'

'Ask me to take a share in raising Harry?'

'This was only our second kiss!'

'I know.' She managed a rueful smile. 'I'm looking at an egg and seeing a dinosaur. Talk about forward cata-strophising. But when you hold me I feel...like it could be the beginning.'

'That makes two of us. Kate, I think I could love you.'

'That's what you say,' she said gently. 'But how can I trust in such a word? It'd fit really neatly for you, wouldn't it? You need a family for Harry. Harry already likes me and he loves Maisie. Replace Annalise with good ol' Kate and your problems are solved.'

Whoa. How had they got here? A kiss and she was projecting forward to marriage, parenthood, delegation of responsibility? This was nuts. But as he looked at her he felt a jolt of recognition in what she was saying.

She was gorgeous. She was an old friend. She was the answer to his problems, wrapped up in one very desir-able package.

Maybe subconsciously she was right.

'Get your house in order,' she said softly. 'Do what you need to do to make you and Harry into a family. Then think of expanding.'

'I'm not kissing you because I want a family!' It was an explosion and she smiled faintly, almost teasingly.

'But are you kissing me because you don't want a family?'

'That's unfair.'

'Unfair or not, I'm taking no chances.' She rose, put-ting physical distance between them. 'I'm your nephew's treating doctor,' she said. 'Kissing you is unprofessional, crossing boundaries that shouldn't be crossed. I need to put those boundaries back into place.'

'We both know that's nonsense.'

'We both know it makes sense. Jack, this needs to stop.'

He rose, too, anger building. She'd built this into something it wasn't. She was insinuating he was manipulating. He wouldn't.

A tiny voice in the back of his head said he might. It would be so easy to give Harry a loving, caring Kate.

Her phone rang.

She'd laid it on the wicker table. All the tension in the room seemed to turn and focus on that table, and maybe that was a relief. How had they reached this point? Kissing had never meant this much before, Jack thought. How had it escalated so fast?

How much easier to focus on a telephone than on the tension zinging between them.

Kate flicked it open. 'It's Alan,' the voice said, audible in the stillness, and Jack recognised it as one of the parents. Wendy's father. The eleven-year-old with the neuroblastoma.

And Kate switched into medical mode, just like that. 'How can I help?'

'Wendy's vomiting,' he said. 'She's getting distressed. Would you—?'

'I'll be there in two minutes.' She disconnected and turned to Jack.

'Harry will be okay,' she said, and he realised she'd turned back into the professional she was. Personal interaction was over. 'You and Harry will make a great family,' she told him. 'You have the skills to help him. Talk to me again if you need to—that's what I'm here for—but between you and me, we're done. I need to fetch my bag and take care of Wendy. Goodnight, Jack. Give Harry a hug for me.'

And he'd been dismissed. She'd finished with one client and she was moving on to another.

CHAPTER NINE

THE NEXT FEW days went well, as far as Harry was concerned. Every day he woke up brighter, more voluble, embracing life again. He had his reassurance from Jack, and even more than the dolphin therapy it seemed to make a difference. He turned to Jack over and over—'Jack, watch me. Jack, can we do this? Jack, get up, Hobble's waiting. Jack, I don't like spaghetti.'

It seemed Jack had turned into a parent, just like that. It left Jack feeling confounded, maybe even trapped, but as he saw the difference it was making to Harry he could only feel relief.

He couldn't want it any other way, but still there was the sensation of walls closing around him. It seemed he was a family, like it or not.

A single parent.

'You'll manage,' Kate said to him on the third or fourth day after that last kiss, and he wondered if his face was so revealing.

'Of course I will.'

'Even without a woman,' she said, and chuckled. He watched her head back to the dolphin pool and felt—on top of everything else—a gut-wrenching sense of loss.

If he'd done things differently he might...

What? Have Kate for a wife? Have a mother for Harry? Bind Kate to the solution he had to find?

It wasn't fair. He accepted that. What was between them had escalated far too fast, and he understood her fear. But he watched her with her little patients, he saw the care and the kindness, he heard her laughter, he watched her tease, cajole, empathise, and he wondered why he hadn't seen this all those years ago.

Was it because he'd never thought of wanting a permanent partner—a partner in the real sense of the word? Was it because he'd never wanted anyone to share his life?

And he was honest enough now to accept that he couldn't differentiate his needs. Yes, Kate was seeming more and more desirable, but he knew Harry was in the equation, too, and he couldn't lay that on her.

Maybe in the future…

Ha. In the future he'd be in Sydney and she'd still be here. She was treating him with professional distance now. How could putting the width of Australia between them make anything different?

'Jack, watch me. Jack, I can swim eighteen whole strokes before Kate has to put her hand under my tummy. Jack, Hobble pushed my tummy up even before Kate reached me.'

Woman and dolphins were an amazing medical team, he thought as he made admiring noises and tried not to make eye contact with Kate—because making eye contact with Kate seemed to make things harder. More convoluted. More needy. He tried to focus on his nephew's achievements and they were indeed awesome.

Someone should write up what she was achieving in the medical journals, he thought, but then he thought of the shadows in Kate's past and he knew such a thing was impossible.

Besides, there weren't enough dolphins in the world to do what Hobble and his mates were achieving. He'd been truly lucky to find this place.

To find Kate?

And it always seemed to come back to Kate. She was racing Harry now—or pretending to race him. They each had a cork kickboard and they were kicking to the side of the pool.

Hobble was zooming between them, creating a wake, heading Kate off so she had to change direction just as she got a lead. Harry was laughing so hard he was almost forgetting to kick—but kick he was, with his injured leg, putting aside pain as unimportant.

This was miracle territory. Hobble and his mates were miracle-makers.

So was Kate, but she was a woman alone and he needed to respect that.

At two the next morning he woke to a knock on the bungalow door. It was such a light knock he might have dreamed it, but years of medicine had given him a knack of sleeping lightly. He was out of bed even before the knocking stopped.

He flung the door wide and Kate was in front of him. She was wearing her customary jeans and a windcheater, and her curls had been tugged back into a loose knot. She looked as if she'd woken in a hurry and rushed out.

Her feet were bare. He looked at her in the moonlight and thought...he thought he'd better not go there.

'Jack, could you help me?' she said, and emotion and desire took a back seat as he switched to medicine. The professional side of him was awake and alert and ready to act.

'Of course.' No hesitation. After all she'd done for Harry, whatever this woman asked of him, she had it.

'It's Wendy,' she said. 'You know she has neuroblastoma. It started in the adrenal glands but she presented late. Her parents put tiredness and weight loss down to puberty. They were busy, they have three other kids and they just didn't notice. So it's already metastasised, with spread into the abdomen and the liver. She's been through twelve months of intensive treatment, with chemo and radiation targeting each tumour, but she's run out of options.'

'So what's happening now?' Two weeks ago he would have asked what a child with such a diagnosis was doing in a place like this, but that had been before he'd got to know Kate and her miracle-workers. All he needed was a medical status update.

'She's vomiting. She had an episode four nights back—that was when you and I...' She paused, and her colour mounted a bit but she had herself under control in an instant. 'I got things under control then, but tonight she's vomiting again and she's worse. I've given her promethazine and set up an IV line for fluids but she's not settling. Jack, I'm out of options. If you can't help I need to get a chopper in and transfer her to Perth.'

'Is that what her parents want?'

'They're desperate for her to stay here,' she said simply. 'After twelve months of hospitals and intensive treatment, she's had enough. She came in three weeks ago, traumatised and almost as withdrawn as Harry after months of coping with frightened adults, but here she's turned into a kid again. She's loving it, and we're fighting to have her stay as long as we can. But I can't stop her vomiting. Jack, you're an oncologist. I hate asking—you're here as a client as well—but if you would take a look...'

'Of course I will.' There was no hesitation. But then he glanced back toward Harry's bedroom. Problem. He was a single dad. He wasn't free to leave.

But once again Kate was ahead of him.

'I've woken Louise,' she said. 'If you agree to help,

she'll be here in two minutes to take over Harry duty. She's great at this sleep business. She'll be on your sofa, snoozing as if we hadn't even woken her, two minutes after she gets here, but she'll hear the slightest sound from Harry. It's a splinter skill she's proud of. Let her show it off.'

And there was nothing else to say.

'Give me ten seconds to haul on jeans and T-shirt,' he told her. 'Kate, I make no promises. There's every chance Wendy will need to be evacuated to get decent symptom control but I'll see what I can do.'

She'd known Jack was good back in med. school. It took all of five minutes of watching him with Wendy and that knowledge was confirmed. He had the empathy and he had the skills to match.

Wendy was exhausted and sick and frightened. Her parents were terrified.

It took a whole thirty seconds with Jack to calm them down.

'Hi,' he said, as she showed him into the little cabin, into Wendy's bedroom where her parents were standing by the bed, looking like deer trapped in headlights. 'Hey, Wendy, Dr Kate tells me you can't stop being sick. Is it okay with you if I see if I can help? Dr Kate's good—she and I went to university together so I know she's about the best doctor around—but while she specialised in family medicine I specialised in caring for people who have cancer. People like you, Wendy. That means right now I have skills that might help.'

He was talking straight to Wendy. It was the right thing to do. Wendy's parents straightened a little, and she could see the sliver of hope lessening their despair. Courtesy of Jack.

'How long since you've been sick?' Jack asked.

'Five…about five minutes,' her mum said haltingly, and Jack gave her a smile that said, excellent, he obviously had another professional on side. And the sliver of hope intensified.

'That's good. This awful retching usually goes in about twenty-minute cycles so we have a window of time to get this sorted. Let's see what we can do before the next one hits. Wendy, I might not be able to stop the next couple of vomits but I should be able to stop them after that. Is it okay with you if I try? Can I take a look at your tummy?'

'Yes,' Wendy quavered.

'You must be tired of doctors,' he said. 'But I have one advantage. I have very warm hands.'

'Wh-why are they warm?'

'I have hot blood,' he said smugly. 'I've trained it. Some people can touch their foreheads with their toes. I can warm up my hands on command. Want to feel?'

'Yes,' Wendy said, and Kate almost gasped. Ten minutes ago the atmosphere in this room had been one of despair. Now not only was there hope, there was a touch of fascination. A blood-warming specialist…

Jack was moving fast, with light banter, as he lifted Wendy's pyjama top. His hands probed gently. Kate knew what he'd be feeling—an enlarged liver in her distended tummy, a hard, appalling mass of unmovable tumour.

'I don't suppose you have an X-ray machine lying around here someplace?' he asked Kate, as if it didn't matter too much.

But it did matter. If he could diagnose what was going on…

'Yes,' she said. 'Basic films are all I can organise, though. MRIs are out of our league.'

'Basic films are good,' Jack said fine. 'In the main building?'

'Yes.'

'If I wrap you up nice and warm and carry you, will you try very hard not to be sick on me?' Jack said to Wendy. 'If you're going to be sick, call out and I'll give you to your dad to carry. If I'm not mistaken, you had spaghetti for tea and I have my favourite T-shirt on. If you're sick on it I'll look like I'm covered in spaghetti graffiti. I'm cool but not that cool.'

And unbelievably, incredibly, Wendy giggled. 'You're silly,' she managed. 'Everyone says…everyone says you're silly.'

'Yes, but I'm silly and clean,' Jack said, grinning back at her. 'Okay, my lady, let's get you X-rayed. Ready, set, go.'

Kate hadn't bothered with taking X-rays. No matter what they showed she was beyond her level of expertise, but what she saw confirmed what she expected. A complete bowel blockage. That meant evacuation. There was no way she could cope with this here.

But Jack took the X-rays and as they went into her little side office to check them he didn't even suggest evacuation. 'Right,' he snapped. 'What medications do you have? Dexamethasone? Morphine? Sedatives?'

'Yes, but I don't have the skill—'

'I do,' he said. 'This isn't a huge blockage. I'm thinking steroid can reduce the swelling and clear it.'

'But if it doesn't work…'

'It has just as much chance of working here as in Perth. Kate, I'm looking at this mass of tumour and thinking no surgeon's going to operate. One blockage will be followed by another. But if I can get the swelling down we may well buy some time.' He put a hand on her shoulder. 'You know there's no easy answer, Kate, in fact there's no answer at all, but there is a way forward. If we use steroid to ease the swelling and unblock the bowel then she may well have a few good weeks. When things catch up with her, the steroid will be discontinued. Death will be fast. But right now this is a no-brainer in terms of treatment.'

'And you can do this here?'

'Yes,' he said—and she believed him.

Trust was such a nebulous thing. She'd sworn not to trust but as she looked up at his face, as she felt the strength of his hand on her shoulder, she felt trust sweep over her. Stupid or not, she trusted this man.

And not just as a doctor.

She nodded. He gave her a smile that said he understood the mix of emotions swirling in her head and for some reason she trusted that, too.

And then it was time to face Wendy. Her parents had taken her back to their cabin. She'd just copped another bout of retching and was limp in her dad's arms but she was still awake and aware. Her mum was sitting to the side, looking as ill as her daughter.

The little girl looked beyond exhaustion but Jack still talked directly to her. 'Wendy, what Dr Kate and I can see in the X-rays is lots of fluid. That's why your tummy feels so hard. It tells me you have a blockage in your tummy so the food you've been eating can't move through. So you have a choice. The doctors who looked after you before you came here could look after you again—Dr Kate says we can organise a helicopter to take you to Perth—but Dr Kate tells me you'd like to stay here. If that's what you want, then you need to trust me to care for you. Is that okay?'

And he didn't need to go further. Kate had told him that Wendy's parents had been warned of potential problems like this before they'd come here. Spelling those problems out now would terrify their daughter. He could take them outside and talk, but Wendy had had a year of medical procedures and lots of bad news. She'd have figured by now what doctors taking her parents outside meant.

So now Jack was treating Wendy as the decision-maker, and Kate could feel the family's trust in him grow stronger. Trust…it seemed to be growing by the moment.

'What can you do?' Wendy's father growled, and Kate could see the big man trying not to cry.

'Stop the vomiting,' Jack said promptly. 'Dr Kate tells me we have steroid here, and morphine.'

'I like morphine,' Wendy murmured, and Kate felt ill at the thought of the mass of the procedures and illness this little girl had endured to make her say such a thing. No child this age should even know what morphine was. But Jack was smiling. He was good, this man. He was exuding confidence, and it was making everyone relax.

'I'll bet you do, and for good reason because it's good at making you feel better. I'll give you steroid, too. That'll make the swelling in your tummy go down, and the vomiting will stop. Wendy, if it's okay with you, I'll give you something now to make you go to sleep. That'll make your tummy relax while we slip in the drugs that'll make the swelling go down. If you and me and your tummy all co-operate, I think you might be back in the pool with Hobble by tomorrow.'

'You're kidding.' Wendy's father's words were an explosion of disbelief. Minutes earlier they'd been facing evacuation to Perth with no promise of any real improvement at the end of it. Now they were being promised… dolphins?

'I'm not joking.' Jack met his disbelief head on. 'I would never joke about Wendy's tummy.' Then, as the man veered between distrust and hope, he put a hand on his shoulder. 'I'm an oncologist,' he said. 'Treating problems like Wendy's is what I do. I can see what's wrong on the X-rays and I know how to fix it.' He glanced again Wendy, and the look Wendy returned was that of a kid older than her years. Be honest, Kate pleaded silently, and he was.

'This isn't a long-term cure,' he said. 'Wendy, you know you still have cancer. But I can make you better for now. What do you say, Wendy? Will you let me make you feel better?'

'Yes,' Wendy whispered, and because she was a polite child she added a rider. 'Yes, please.'

It sounded easy but it wasn't easy. Even sedated, the involuntary retching continued. The steroid took time to work, and there was a real risk of dehydration and exhaustion simply making her body shut down.

But she wasn't ready to die yet. If they were lucky, Kate thought as the night wore on, blockage wouldn't be the cause of death. She could have a few good weeks courtesy of the steroid, and if the fates were kind she could simply drift peacefully away.

That was what Jack was fighting for. Time, but more than time—a chance for her parents to be able to say goodbye to their daughter without the gut-wrenching awfulness of watching their daughter's distress.

Kate stayed as Jack administered dexamethasone subcutaneously. She didn't doubt him. His skill as he injected the steroid was matched only by his gentleness. He gave haloperidol for the nausea and she watched with him until the retching stopped, until the little girl's body finally relaxed into sleep, until the steroid had a chance to start working.

Even then he wouldn't leave. She would have taken over—it was simply a matter of keeping the little girl's airway clear, keeping the obs up—but when she offered, Jack shook his head.

'I'm physician in charge,' he growled. 'If Louise is happy to care for Harry...'

'She is.'

'Then you have patients to treat in the morning and I don't. Go to bed, Kate, and leave Wendy to me.'

She didn't want to leave.

There was no need for her to stay. Wendy was asleep. Her parents were asleep, too, on the armchairs just through the door, but she knew the slightest noise would rouse them.

They slept, however, because they trusted Jack to take care of their daughter.

She could do the same.

But...but...

She didn't want to leave...him?

'Bed,' he said gently, and he raised a hand and ran his finger lightly down her cheek. It was a feather touch, the slightest of caresses that should have meant nothing but in truth meant everything.

'Jack, thank you...'

'It's my job.'

'You came here to be treated yourself.'

'I brought Harry for treatment.'

'Treatment here is for the whole family,' she said. 'That's what you and Harry are. A family.'

'And what about you, Kate?' he asked softly. 'Where's a family for you?' And then he smiled, that warm, endearing smile that made her heart do back flips.

'That's not a question to be answered tonight,' he said. 'Tonight's for sleeping. But in the morning...next month...next year... You're too precious a person to stay alone. I won't let that bastard scar you for ever. But go to sleep, my Kate. Let's worry about tomorrow tomorrow.'

* * *

She left and Jack was left with the sleeping Wendy. The night stretched on. Every now and then Wendy stirred and Jack checked, making sure her breathing was secure, keeping her safe.

Why? It was a question he asked himself often as an oncologist. Many of his patients were facing inevitable death. Why prolong it?

Because life was good.

He'd always believed it—sort of—but tonight that belief was suddenly intensified. Why?

Because he'd touched Kate's face? Because he'd seen the change in her expression that said she trusted him, and there was hope in that look.

So many factors were coming into play. He had the long night to think about them, and think about them he did.

The unhappiness of his parents' marriage, pushing him to turn into himself.

The loss of his little sister.

Harry's dependence.

A man could lose hope, he thought, but as he watched the gentle rise and fall of Wendy's chest, he knew that the opposite was true.

Hope was all there was, he thought.

And trust.

Kate trusted him. For some reason the thought was almost overwhelming. It was a gift beyond measure.

Not to be taken lightly.

Not to be rushed.

The night wore on. As the first rays of a breaking dawn showed through the curtains, Wendy's sleep settled. The tension on her face faded. He felt her tummy and listened and heard unmistakeable bowel sounds.

Things were moving. The steroid was starting to do its job.

She'd have time.

How much time?

Did it matter? he thought. A day, a month, a year, a lifetime. He'd take everything he could get and make it good.

Was this about him or Wendy?

Both of them, he thought, tucking the bedclothes back around the little girl's body. Right now he felt almost a part of her.

'Any man's death diminishes me, because I am involved with mankind.'

Donne's words... He'd heard them, he'd even said them to himself as he'd fought for patient after patient over the years, but now they seemed clearer.

He was fighting for Wendy. He was involved.

He was involved with Harry in a way that couldn't be undone.

He wanted to be involved with Kate.

And isolation? The desire to stand apart so he couldn't be hurt? Where was that now?

Dissolved, he thought, or maybe it had never existed. Maybe it was something he could never achieve because Beth had always been there, and then Harry, and his patients like Wendy.

And Kate...

He wasn't sure where to take this.

'But I will try,' he told the sleeping Wendy. 'For your sake. For all our sakes. Life's too short and too precious. For now let's get out there and play with some dolphins. Let's let ourselves love. Let's give everything we have.'

Wendy stirred again but this time it wasn't a movement of discomfort. It was just a child stirring in normal sleep.

'You stay well,' he told her. 'For as long as you have. Let's grab life with both hands, Wendy, girl. While we can.'

CHAPTER TEN

WENDY RECOVERED, AND something had healed inside Kate as well. For some crazy reason she felt she'd recovered with her.

But maybe this recovery was just like Wendy's, she told herself. Wendy's cure was short term. She was splashing in the dolphin pool, lying in a rubber ring, being pushed around the pool by the dolphins, weak but happy. She seemed to be soaking up every moment of this respite, and maybe that was because it *was* a respite. They all knew her cancer was waiting in the wings, pushed back for now but still there.

Maybe Kate's distrust was still there as well, but some time during the night of Wendy's illness she'd put it aside.

Jack was here now. She was trusting him.

She was loving him?

There was a question.

To all the world he was simply another parent. After the night with Wendy he'd reverted to being Harry's guardian, Harry's carer, Harry's playmate. But things had changed with him, too, she thought. He'd relaxed in his relationship with Harry. He no longer seemed reserved. Harry was turning into a normal little boy. He was still quiet but maybe he'd always be quiet. He was gaining in confidence, the strain had gone from his eyes and he seemed confident of his world again.

'I read on the internet about tame dolphins,' he told Kate at the end of a session where he'd pushed his injured leg to the limit, so much so that Kate had called a halt and made him slow down. 'It says it's really cruel to keep them in enclosures.'

'There are people who think that,' Kate said gravely. They were sitting in the shallows, watching Hobble and his mates toss balls to each other. 'They're the ones who say we should let nature take its course. We could open the gates now, Hobble and his mates would be free—but the experts tell us that with their background and their injuries they'd be dead within weeks. There are people who say that's better than them being in captivity. I don't know. What do you think?'

She was talking to Harry as she would to an adult. Jack sat in the shallows beside them and listened. This was what Harry wouldn't get if he went to live with Helen, he thought. Helen treated her kids as kids. Helen and Doug had brought them up on baby talk. Beth and Arthur had explained scientific theories to Harry before he could talk back.

'I don't want them to die,' Harry said cautiously. 'But the internet said it's wrong for humans to treat them as play things.'

He was seven years old. Jack blinked. This kid astonished him more and more.

As did Kate. He waited for her to say it was silly. After all this was a defence of everything she worked for, but instead she gazed out at the dolphins and took her time to answer.

'I've thought about that,' she said at last. 'A lot. I studied this place carefully before I came to work here. I'm not sure whether my decision is right but here's the premise I'm working on.'

Premise... It was a big word for a seven-year-old but

Harry didn't blink. He knew the word. He was a scientist at seven.

And Jack felt a sudden swell of pride that had nothing to do with the fact that this was his nephew and Beth's son and he was his guardian. It was everything to do with Harry as a person.

It'd be a privilege to raise this kid, he thought, and then he caught Kate's glaze. She smiled and he thought, She knows what I'm thinking.

Drat, he didn't do emotion.

He was doing emotion now.

'My thinking is that these dolphins have been saved,' Kate said. 'It's very hard to see an injured or orphaned dolphin and not help it. The argument for and against saving them is hard, and I and the people who work here don't have control over it. All we do is take rescued dolphins and care for them. And caring for them means not letting them get bored. We've given them a ginormous enclosure but that's not enough. In the wild these guys would surf and catch fish and swim for miles. So we figure they need toys. That's what you are. A toy.'

'A toy?' Harry asked, fascinated.

'Exactly.' She beamed. 'You may think you're lucky getting to play with the dolphins but think of it from the dolphins' point of view. Every day we give them a different set of toys to play with. One of them's called Harry.'

Harry thought about it. He thought about it deeply, his small face a picture of concentration.

Kate said nothing.

She really was the most restful of women, Jack thought. She really was...

Um, no. Not yet. There was no way he could rush what was becoming blindingly obvious.

This was too precious to rush.

'So it's like giving Hobble a toy train,' Harry said—

cautiously. 'Only instead of a toy train you're giving him a Harry.'

'Exactly,' Kate said, and beamed some more. 'We cover you up with a blue skin suit so you can't damage the dolphins with sunscreen. We give you the rules and we let the dolphins play with you. And they know that every blue-wrapped gift is different. They figure it out. Watch how they treat Sam and his swimming—they know he's strong in the upper body, they know he loves to swim. See how they react to Susie jumping up and down. They seem to jump, too. Watch how they nudge Wendy round the pool in her water ring. They never frighten her. Watch how they tease you, every day trying to make you swim faster. I don't think it's cruel to let them play with you, Harry. I think they love it.'

'But they're still stuck.'

'They are still stuck,' she agreed. 'They've all been permanently injured in some way and there's nothing we can do to fix that. So they're stuck like Sam's stuck in his wheelchair, but there are so many ways they can still have fun, just like Sam still has fun.'

Silence. Harry considered some more, and finally his grave little face cracked into a smile.

'I think they need their toy called Harry again,' he said, and chuckled and tossed a ball out onto the water, whooped as dolphins leapt to catch it and headed out into the water to join them.

Leaving Kate and Jack together.

They sat in more silence for a while. They were watching Harry and the dolphins, only they weren't just watching. There were so many undercurrents...so many things waiting to be said.

'That pretty much describes you,' Jack said at last, feeling he was walking on eggshells. But he wanted to get close to this woman. It was so important...

'What does?'

'Injured and stuck.'

'I'm not…' But she faltered and looked away.

Time to probe, he thought. Dared he?

'What would happen if the gates opened and you were free?' he asked, feeling like this was eggshell territory.

'I'd be terrified,' she admitted. 'I've been there. This suits me.'

'For ever?'

'For as long as I can stay hidden.'

'When a dolphin's cured, you do open the gates.'

'Yes, but—'

'But you don't think you'll ever be cured?'

'Maybe not. You think I'm a coward?'

'I don't think anything of the kind, but I do think you could use help. Like you're helping everyone else.'

'I'm happy as I am.'

He motioned out to Hobble. 'So if he had the choice— fix his scarring and join his mates out to sea or stay here for ever—what do you think he'd choose?'

'It's a big world out there.'

'And dangerous. But for him to swim for miles, catch his own fish, do his own thing…'

'I'm doing good here,' she snapped.

'Yes, you are, but the boundaries are still there and they worry you.'

'I have enough to keep me occupied.'

'What about me?' he asked into the stillness. 'I'm on the outside, Kate.'

'I don't know what you mean.'

'I mean I think I'm falling in love with you.'

She drew in her breath and stared out to sea for a while. Refusing to look at him. 'You just want a mother for Harry.'

'That's not true, and you know it.'

'It has to be true, Jack. I'm not in the market for a relationship.'

'Neither am I,' he said softly. 'But, Kate, the way I feel about you...I've never felt this way before. I've been running scared, too. My parents' relationship left me soured, thinking isolation was the way to go. That's how it's been all my life, holding myself contained. I never took a risk like you took with Simon. All my girlfriends have been just that—friends. I don't think I've ever hurt anyone. The women I've dated have all valued their independence as well. But you... Suddenly that independence doesn't seem so important. In fact, it seems crazy to want it. Loving you might entail risks but wouldn't the risks be worth it?'

She did turn to face him then, her eyes troubled. 'Jack, don't.'

'Why not?' he asked gently. 'Why not say it like it is?'

'Because it's too...pat,' she retorted. 'I can't believe it. Independent Jack Kincaid, having his pick of beautiful women, never committing, then suddenly landed with his orphaned nephew. I know you've fallen in love with Harry. I also know how much Harry will change your life—unless you find someone else to share the loving. Who else but Kate? Kate, who's been blackmailed all her life to love, whether she wants it or not.'

There was silence at that. He didn't know where to take it. How to change a woman's faith in the world? How to even begin?

The problem was that no matter how attracted he was to her, Harry was in the equation as well. The vision of a home with Harry and Kate was a thousand times more appealing than a home with just Harry.

A thousand times easier? Kate would make Harry a great mother. She understood him. Was part of his subconscious wanting that?

'See,' Kate said bleakly. 'You can't deny it.'

'I think I can,' he told her. 'Kate, I should have fought for you years ago. You're the most beautiful, the bravest, the best…'

'But you didn't,' she threw back at him. 'Because you didn't have Harry.'

'No,' he admitted. 'And Harry's changed me. I hardly understand what that change is all about either. I agree I'm struggling. But what I feel for you…'

'Needs to be tempered with sense. What you're struggling with is a good dose of panic at being a single dad.'

'I don't think I am,' he said, looking out at Harry. 'I want to do this.'

'Then do it,' she said. 'And in a year or so come back and see me—if you still want to.'

'You'll still be in your enclosure?'

'Leave it,' she said roughly, rising to her feet. 'Let it be, Jack. I'm happy here and it's taken all my life to get this happy. Please don't mess with it.'

'I won't,' he said, and he didn't rise to stand by her. He let her be, even if it nearly killed him. 'It's your call, Kate. You're right, my life is being turned upside down. All I know is what I feel. How can I trust that? I'm not sure I can, but I need to try. Let me know if you do, too.'

'I'm fine as I am,' Kate said.

'I'm sure you are,' Jack said. 'But I'm also sure you'd like to be free. But the way you're feeling…asking you to love me might be asking you to go from one enclosure to another and I'd never do that to you. Just know that if you ever want it, Harry and I will be waiting for you. Waiting to be free together.'

There was a lot there for a woman to think about—almost too much. Luckily the rest of the day's sessions were straightforward. The dolphins did their stuff, the kids didn't push injured limbs too far, the day was gorgeous, the mums and the dads were happy—all was right in her world.

Except Jack loved her.

What was wrong with that?

It scared her witless. It made her want to run.

Why?

Because a part of her—a really big part—said giving in to love left her exposed, as she'd been for most of her life. Love was gossamer chains that, when tugged against, became spiked steel.

Maybe she was being stupid, she conceded. She was comparing the love Jack was offering to the suffocating love of her parents—and to what Simon called love, the love of greed and cruelty.

But still...it was too much of a coincidence, she told herself, and she knew it was true. Jack had been left to care for his injured nephew. She'd formed a bond with Harry. Jack knew, or at least he must guess, how much she'd love to care for such a child as her own, and Jack needed that commitment. Because if she committed, he wouldn't have to.

Her parents had loved her because they'd needed her. Simon had 'loved' her because he'd wanted control and money. And here was Jack, who needed a mother for his child.

But it was more than that. She could trust Jack.

How? She didn't know, but there was somehow a deep sense that seemed to be working by instinct, that watched him up the beach now as he dug holes with his nephew, that said here was a man she could trust with her life.

But there was another part of her, the part that had been on the run for years, the part that had been battered and broken by a dreadful marriage, and that part said she was a fool. Had she learned nothing?

If Jack had come to her without Harry then...

No. Not even then. Trust had to be absolute, and how could she ever leave herself vulnerable?

She wanted to head somewhere and weep.

She wanted to lay it all out in front of Jack and let him tell her it was nonsense.

Instead, she bounced in the water and cheered on her little clients, and as she worked with each of them she thought of the shocking paths that had brought each of them here. Life was cruel. Random.

You had to protect yourself, she thought, and suddenly Maisie was lunging down the beach, through the shallows to reach her like, beaching herself on her mistress like she'd found her very own island. She was landed with an armful of soaking golden retriever. Maisie wriggled and licked and dripped and Kate thought this was the kind of treatment Maisie reserved for her very neediest of patients.

So why her? Why now?

Because she needed her. She hugged back and if she sniffed back a tear it was hidden in the fur of soaked dog. Finally she pulled away, and smiled and looked back to where Matilda Everingham was using her one good arm to try and keep a ball out of Hobble's reach.

Matilda was recovering from a car accident. This place was helping her recover.

Like it was helping *her* recover.

'And you can't recover by jumping from the frying pan straight back into the fire,' she told herself, and glanced again at the man and the boy on the beach. 'They need you but so does everyone else here. I won't let love blackmail me into anything.'

Yet...Harry was earnestly telling something to his uncle. Jack laughed and hugged his little nephew and the sight did something to her insides.

She could be part of it.

Yeah. And she'd be left keeping the home fires burning, taking over Jack's domestic responsibilities, and Jack would go back to the life he knew. *She could not trust.*

'And that's the end of it,' she said, turning back to Matilda and trying to edge aside her soggy dog. 'Thanks for the hugs, Maisie, but stick around. I just might need more of them.'

So much for taking things slowly. He'd scared her witless. She thought he was wanting a mother for Harry.

Maybe he did. Maybe her doubts were justified. He spent the next couple of days trying to give her space, while he tried to sort out his own thoughts.

A couple of days didn't help. Or maybe they did. Every time he saw her he became more and more sure that what he was feeling had nothing to do with Harry.

His thoughts kept drifting back to the night of that student party all those years ago, when Beth had floated home after meeting Arthur. His normally quiet, reserved little sister had been glowing.

'I can't tell you... I can't explain... All I know is that he's the one. If I'm wrong I'll break my heart but he seems to feel it, too. Oh, Jack, I don't believe in them but I seem to be in the middle of a miracle.'

Her joy had left him confused and concerned. What was she letting herself in for? How had it happened? Maybe if Arthur had looked like the next James Bond he'd have understood, but Arthur had been a bespectacled, mild-mannered man who'd looked at his sister as if he'd been granted his own miracle.

And now he was looking at Kate and feeling exactly the same.

But it wasn't reciprocated. Kate was running scared, and with reason.

So what to do?

In the end he decided he simply didn't know, but one thing was sure, nothing could happen here. He was the guardian of one of Kate's patients. She was treating him with professional detachment and he had to accept that. Pushing boundaries would not only be unfair on Kate, it could very well jeopardise Harry's recovery.

So wait.

Until when?

He didn't know. He and Harry were only booked here for another couple of days.

Still, he had to wait.

Waiting was easier said than done, but he did have things to do to fill in the time.

He was thinking of his life in Sydney as it had been. On call twenty-four seven. Living and breathing for his career.

He was thinking of his life as it now had to be, if he was to fit a small boy into it. No, he thought as he worked through priorities. He didn't need to fit Harry into his life. His life and Harry's had to merge. Two lives, equal priorities.

With Kate…three?

He couldn't ask her. Not yet. He got it, he thought. She'd been controlled for so long that for him to assume the control was his had been…cruel. He didn't know how to fix it. He only knew, for now, he needed to focus on Harry.

So for now his focus was total.

He had a life to reorganise. He had a family to make, including Kate or not.

CHAPTER ELEVEN

SATURDAY. LATE MORNING. Harry was Kate's last client before lunch. Up until two days ago Jack had joined them in the water, but for the last couple of days he'd pleaded a need to get work done. But it wasn't true. He'd done everything he needed to get his life after Dolphin Bay sorted. For now he had time to sit on the beach and watch a vibrant, loving woman encourage his nephew to do things no one could have imagined him doing two weeks ago.

She was a miracle-worker. Harry's bad leg kicked now with full extension. What's more, almost the whole time in the water he chatted. He'd never be the most voluble of kids, but he answered questions and he asked his own.

'Tell Hobble what you want him to do,' Kate told him, and the little boy considered the dolphin and set him a challenge.

'I want you to swim all the way round the pool before I get to the edge,' he decreed, and Jack grinned at the little boy's school teacherly tone. Also the task he'd set him. The pool was vast in circumference and they were fifteen yards from the edge. But Harry started swimming, and Kate whistled. Hobble zoomed round the pool like lightning, Harry splashed in a frenzy to the side of the pool and they arrived together. Harry surfaced nose to nose with the dolphin, crowing with delight. 'I almost beat you.'

'I don't believe it.'

He'd been so entranced an entire battalion could have sneaked up behind him. It wasn't a battalion. It was scarier. His sister-in-law was standing on the sandhill behind him. Helen.

Helen wasn't looking at him. She was staring out at Harry.

'Oh, my,' she murmured. 'Oh, Jack, look.'

'He's good, isn't he?' As astounded as he was by her visit, his pride rang out clear and true. 'Two weeks and he's a new man.'

But Helen was already running down the sand, calling out to the pair in the water. 'Harry. Harry, it's Aunty Helen. Oh, Harry…'

Jack watched as Harry froze. Kate was beside him. She put her hand on his shoulder and bent and said something, and Harry's shoulders braced. Who knew what Kate had said but whatever it was it seemed to have worked. Kate took his hand and together they waded from the water. Harry was promptly enveloped in a giant aunt-hug. Then Maisie bounded along the beach. Of course she did. Visitors and Maisie not on hand to welcome them was an unheard-of phenomenon. Aunt, kid and dog became one gigantic cuddle.

Jack grinned, but then he thought, Why is she here? To take Harry home?

The hug was separating into its component parts. Helen took Harry's hand, whether he willed it or not, and led him up the beach. Jack saw Kate hesitate and he sent her his very best pleading look. She hesitated a bit longer, eyeing the group unenthusiastically, then gave a rueful smile and a shrug and came.

He was a stronger man with Kate behind him, he thought. Or should that be in front?

'Hey,' Helen said, releasing Harry for a moment to give Jack a hug. 'You're a magician.'

'It's Kate who's the magician,' Jack said mildly. 'Kate, this is Harry's aunt, Helen.'

'So you're the hunted wife,' Helen said, and Jack winced. How many people had Helen told?

'I'm Harry's counsellor and physiotherapist,' Kate said, carefully calm. 'Harry, I'll leave you to your family reunion.'

But Helen stopped her leaving. 'Is Harry ready to go home?' she asked. 'What he's doing with his legs…that's fantastic. And Jack says he's talking. He's healed?'

'We've been talking of going home, haven't we, Harry?' Kate said, and the little boy nodded. Mutely. He wasn't sure what was going on and he wasn't prepared to commit himself.

'We have two more full days,' Jack said.

'I'd rather take him home earlier if it's possible,' Helen told him, briskly efficient. 'Doug's looking after the children for the weekend but he needs to be back at work on Monday. If we could take Harry tomorrow, that would be splendid. Jack, when you were dubious about this place you told me your airfares from Perth are flexible. Annalise has told me you two are splitting up. I've thought about it and I've decided it'd be best if we go home together, giving Harry time to adjust to me.'

What followed was silence. A very long silence. Kate stayed still and watchful. Helen was smiling, expecting assent to her plans. Harry stood mute, staring down at the sand. Into the stillness Maisie crept, pressing firmly against Harry. It was as if she sensed she was needed.

Kate took a couple of steps back but she didn't leave

them. Jack was looking...tense. His look had been a plea for her to stay. Why?

This was none of her business. She should go—but she was riveted to where she stood.

'It would be good if we could fly home together,' Jack said at last, choosing his words with care. 'It's great of you to offer, Helen, but I've promised Harry we're staying until Tuesday. I don't break promises.' He hesitated. 'And he probably doesn't need time to adjust to you. He'll be living with me.'

'Well, that's dumb,' Helen said. 'That's why I'm here. I know you're being sentimental but sentimentality doesn't come into it. It's crazy to think you can fit childcare around your career. Harry'll fit into my tribe so easily we'll hardly notice. You know we can love him, Jack, and you know you can't.'

Harry studied the sand some more. Kate found she was holding her breath. Could she breathe? She seemed to have forgotten how.

Jack looked at Helen for a long moment and then he looked at down at his small nephew. He stepped forward and swung Harry up into his arms. And held.

'I thought we'd agreed, Helen,' he said, quite lightly. 'Harry's a bit of a loner. He likes quiet and having his own space. He and I get on together. You have your five kids. I have Harry. We can organise things around my career.'

'But Annalise said...' Helen started.

'What did Annalise say?' Once again, he spoke lightly but behind his words Kate sensed steel.

'That you can't manage him together. She's not prepared to take him on. She says it's breaking up your relationship.'

They shouldn't be having this discussion in front of

Harry, Kate thought, but Jack had the little boy in his arms and he wasn't letting go.

'Our relationship,' Jack said, just as lightly but still with that undercurrent of steel, 'has already broken up.'

'Only because of the child.'

Harry had pretty much gone limp. His head was burrowed into Jack's shoulder. She should take him away, Kate thought, but then she decided it wouldn't work. Words had been said that couldn't be unsaid. Harry was bright. He'd have taken in everything. This was all about his future and he was entitled to stay.

'You're on call all the time,' Helen was saying. 'Your career is brilliant but life-consuming. Tell us how that fits with childcare. Even a nanny won't give you the sort of commitment that fits in with your career. You need to find a nice domestic wife and you've never looked like finding one of those.'

A nice domestic wife...

Kate thought again that she'd been right to back away from the magnetic appeal of Jack Kincaid. *Come into my parlour, said the spider to the fly...* What he'd offered had been a sweet and sticky trap. It was another form of the loving she'd been used to—with his needs and manipulation behind it.

But...

'No,' Jack said, deeply and evenly, and she blinked. So did Helen. The word was a resounding negative, a blunt statement, loud and strong, echoing over the sand hills and out to sea.

'What do you mean, no?' Helen said waspishly. 'What are you intending to do? School and after-hours crèche at the hospital? What if he's ill? You're Head of Oncology, Jack, have some sense. I won't let you neglect him.'

'I have no intention of neglecting him. I've quit at Sydney Central.'

'What…?'

'Harry's not the only one who's been doing some heal-ing here,' he told Helen. 'Dr Kate's good. She's been telling me I can't rely on anyone to do what I need to do myself.'

And Kate blinked. What was happening? Instead of reacting angrily to her rejection, he'd changed his course? Surely not.

'Okay, maybe I could find someone,' Jack said, and was she imagining it or did he glance at her? 'As you say, a nice domestic wife. I have no idea how to find one but I dare say I could try. But this isn't anyone's responsibil-ity but mine. Helen, these last two weeks have been time out for me, too, and I've figured a few important things out for myself. First and foremost is that I love Harry. He's my nephew as well as yours. I loved his mum and dad to bits and I love him.'

Wow. That was a biggie for a guy to say. Kate watched the stillness of the little boy's body and knew he was tak-ing in every word.

'Secondly, my work's important,' Jack went on. 'But as I said, these last couple of weeks have been an eye-opener. I've been watching Dr Kate and seeing the amaz-ing work she's doing. I've fought my way through medical circles to be top in my field in oncology. Nothing's been more important than my work, but Kate's shown me that there are different types of important. So, yes, I still want to work in my field but I'm going back to basics.

'I've rung Sydney Central and resigned as Head of Oncology. I've applied for a hands-on position, work-ing at grass-roots level at a town further down the coast. Nothing's firm yet but I'm hoping it comes off. It's a large town rather than a city. There's a need for an oncologist but only one who treats patients directly, and that need's not vast. I'm thinking I can work from nine to four on weekdays. It'll be a huge cut in income, a huge cut in status but it means with the help of a decent housekeeper who's prepared to step in in an emergency, Harry and I can look after each other.'

'But you can't!' Helen was staring at him in stupefaction. 'A rural doctor...you! Jack, what about your research? Even I know how important it is.'

'I can still do that,' Jack said evenly. 'But not as much. As Harry gets older I may be able to pick up the threads of my academic career, but right now that's not what I'm interested in. I'll take care of Harry, and nothing else comes before that.

'It's not like I'm stepping away from my career,' he told her, quite gently because her shock was genuine and she loved Harry, too. 'But there's a community without an oncologist. I treated a kid here the other night...well, you don't need to know the details but it made me realise that grass-roots medicine is still what it's all about. I can treat a community. I can stop many, many cancer sufferers having to go to the city for treatment, and Harry and I can get a life in the process.'

He hugged Harry a bit tighter. 'And there's a beach there too and, amazingly, a dolphin sanctuary,' he added. 'Not like this, it's not a treatment centre, but I figure maybe Harry and I can volunteer to clean pools or something. We're pretty much committed to dolphins now, aren't we, mate?'

And Harry tugged back and looked at his uncle. His face was inches from his. The look that passed between man and boy made something inside Kate twist as it had never twisted before.

'We'll live near dolphins?' Harry whispered.

'Yes.'

'Near a beach?'

'Right near a beach if we can manage it. You'll need to help me hunt for a house.'

She was crying. Stupid, helpless tears were slipping down her face and there wasn't a thing she could do about it.

She'd suspected this man of trying to manipulate her to solve his problems. She might have known he'd do no such thing.

And then she thought…she thought… *He didn't want her to make the problem go away.*

What was happening in her head? Her thoughts were a confused jumble, but through the weird mist she could see a flicker of light. Hope?

Maybe…just maybe he'd like her to join him while they solved problems together.

The thought was huge.

She stood numb while Helen probed Jack's new information, decided she was pleased and hugged Jack and Harry. This family was sorting itself out, she thought. She had a happy ending here. She sniffed and backed off a little. She had more clients waiting.

What was between her and Jack…well, it'd have to wait.

It might not be anything, she conceded. He might indeed have been considering her as the answer to his problems, and then when she'd knocked him back he'd been forced to find another solution.

Maybe he'd talk to her about it. She hoped…

She desperately hoped, she conceded, but now wasn't the time or the place. She was the treating medic. She'd done all she could.

Jack and Harry were still enveloped in Helen's weepy hug. Leave them to it, she told herself, but it took sheer, physical effort to turn away. To turn again into Dr Kate, moving from one client to another.

She did it, though. She sniffed and wished skin suits came with pockets for handkerchiefs. She needed to head for her bungalow before she saw the next client.

She forced herself to turn away, she took two steps... but suddenly Helen broke away from the group hug. She reached her and put a hand on her shoulder and she had to stop and turn.

'Kate,' Helen said. 'C-Cathy?'

She'd met this woman before, a long time ago. Helen had been one of the university crowd, studying pharmacy before dropping out to start a family. She looked at her now and saw the echoes of a wild child who'd seemingly settled contentedly into motherhood. But Helen was looking worried. Was she about to appeal to her to support her?

'This is between you and Jack and Harry,' she said gently. 'I'll leave you to it.'

'It's fine. I mean...I don't really know if it's fine but he's prepared to try...I have to support him,' Helen said. 'But there's something else. I was feeling bad, and then when Doug said I should fly over I thought I should, not just to see Harry but to see you, to see you face to face.'

'Why?'

'Because I think I've blown your cover,' she said bluntly. 'When Jack first got here he asked me about you and I made some enquiries. Then the next day he rang again and told me not to ask around. He said you've been battered and were hiding. So I hoped nothing would come of the enquiries I'd made. But the night before last we got a phone call. From your Simon. He wanted to know all about you. Only he already knows too much. Someone's passed on the stuff I was asking about. He knows where you are, and...well, he sounded vicious. He said he couldn't afford to fly but he'd drive and he'd get here even if it took three days, and he'd make you face up to what you've done. I'm so sorry, Cathy. After all you've done for us…I'm so sorry, but…he's coming.'

'Here?' Kate said, stupidly.

'He made such threats,' Helen said, and her voice told them more than any words could just how terrible those threats had been. 'Doug said we should call the police but I thought…he's driving and it takes three days, so I'd fly. I thought, I'll take Harry home, get him out of here. Then you can phone the police, or leave, or do whatever you have to. Either way, you still have twenty-four hours before he's here.'

CHAPTER TWELVE

SHE'D BEEN FREE for years. Or maybe she hadn't.

The last time she'd seen him Simon had been in court, where she'd outlined the deceits and dishonesty with which he'd destroyed her family and his own. After that she'd had phone calls and emails full of a hate so great it had made her run. She'd changed her name, she'd changed her life, but she knew Simon. She knew wherever she went, his hate would follow.

His hate was bringing him here.

She stared at Helen and she felt like the sand was shifting under her feet.

Simon. Coming here.

She remembered his response when she'd told him she was divorcing him. 'Once my wife, always my wife,' he'd said, and there'd been pure venom behind the words. Venom that had made her skin crawl.

Always my wife... The words made her feel ill.

She'd have to run.

'Kate?' It was Jack. He'd put Harry gently aside, ushering him into Helen's care, and was there beside her. 'There's no need to look like that. We have time to plan to face him. And I *will* be beside you.'

Simon. Coming here.

It was like her world had been knocked off its axis. The fears of years of abuse hadn't gone. She'd buried them but here they were, bursting from deep, dark recesses, making her feel like a kid again, like she had the first time she'd felt his fist.

'Kate.' Jack's hands were on her shoulders. 'Don't look like that. It's okay. This is no threat. You're not alone. You're surrounded by friends.' His hands held her with more strength, forcing her to look at him. 'I will be beside you,' he said again. 'I swear.'

And somehow her terror faltered. Somehow her world steadied.

Why?

Less than a week ago when he'd said he'd keep her safe she'd responded with fear. She hadn't wanted anyone to keep her safe. She hadn't trusted. And she'd had enough of hiding. To stay behind someone...to depend on them for her safety...

But somehow, some way, the promise Jack was making had changed. She reran it in her head, and the terror retreated still further.

I will be beside you.

Those weren't the words of a man who wanted to control her, she thought wildly. Her thoughts were all over the place but they were no longer centred on her ex-husband. They were veering around. They were starting to centre on Jack.

I will be beside you.

Those weren't the words of a man who wanted to manipulate her.

Jack.

They were all watching her—Helen with fear, Harry with worry, Jack with quiet empathy. Empathy. Where had that word come from? Why was it front and centre? Was it because he'd just told Helen what he planned for his life, and those plans didn't include her? Or...they didn't need to include her.

But she could…she might…

What if…?

'Together we'll confront the bastard,' Jack said, quite mildly as it was no big deal at all. 'You have enough medical evidence to put him away all over again. It'll just take courage.'

And there it was again. Jack was offering to help, to stand beside her but not protect her. To stand with her.

It'll just take courage.

She looked around her, at the gorgeous beach, the dolphins, the kids she was helping. Where was her terror taking her? She'd run from this? She'd let Simon drive her from this?

And then she turned and looked at Jack again. His gaze met hers, steady, grave and true. He was giving her space, she thought. He was offering her…something, but her future was hers to decide.

He'd decided his future. He'd planned it without her. He was talking on Harry's care and he was asking no one to share it with him.

But she might… She could…

Her mind was a mass of whirling thoughts, but it was still centring on Jack.

'I don't know where to start,' she faltered, and Jack smiled.

'If you're ready, you can start right now.'

'Ready?'

'To accept help. If you're ready to give statements, Susie's dad is a cop. High ranking. He doesn't look powerful in his sunsuit but he is. A word from us and Simon can be stopped before he even reaches here. If you're prepared to give statements…'

Then he paused. He let her thoughts take her where she willed. No pressure, his silence said. The future was hers to choose.

So many thoughts…

What had Jack said all those nights ago when he'd seen the scar on her arm? *There's no statute of limitations on assault charges.* She thought of the litany of assaults she'd had at Simon's hands. She thought of the medical evidence she could show.

It took courage. It was easier to run.

'If you say the word, I will be beside you.' He said it again gently, and the terror had receded enough for her to hear the vow behind the words. It was as if a blanket had been put around her, a fleece of strength and comfort.

And love?

And she thought again of what Jack was prepared to do. Stand aside from his career. Give up his home, his friends, the world he knew, so he could take on the care of one small boy.

She thought, wildly, that if he could, maybe she could too.

'It'd have to work both ways,' she whispered, and she thought he wouldn't hear, but he did. His eyes warmed, gleamed, and his gaze caressed her.

'That could be arranged,' he said, and he smiled, and Helen stared at them both.

'What are you two on about?'

'Decisions,' Jack said. 'Holding each other up. The whole being greater than its parts.'

'You're not making sense. Shall I call the police?'

But Kate didn't want the police. Not yet. Not when such an important sensation was swirling…

Hope…

She shook her head. 'I… Not yet. There's time.'

'There is,' Jack said, his eyes still on hers. His smile was a little quizzical, like he hoped he'd guessed right but he wasn't sure.

But she was sure. Or she was as sure as she could be.

She looked around her once again, at the beach, at her dolphins, at this place of healing. Jack would stand by her while she defended herself, she knew. He'd fight for her right to stay here.

But he was moving to another life. Her mind had been whirling but his smile was settling her. Showing her true north.

'You will be free,' he said, gently, lovingly? 'We'll get details of every injury. We'll outline the steps you've taken to run from him. We'll also have Helen outline the threats he made to her. Given his history, his past convictions, we can see him in jail for a very long time.'

'G-good.'

'There's no need to run. You can do whatever you want.'

Whatever she wanted?

She wanted Jack. She knew it then, surely and truly.

She loved this man with all her heart. She looked at him and she knew. All she needed now was the courage to say it. To ask?

She must. Jack had asked her once to share his life. Now that he was walking away from her life, could he want her still?

To ask seemed almost outrageous but she watched his face and she knew he wouldn't ask himself. She'd accused him of wanting a mother for Harry. She'd thrown it back at him. But now...

'I'd like to be with you,' she said.

'Be...'

'If you'll have me.' She hesitated. Was she misreading his touch, the way he was looking at her? She hoped not. With all her heart, she hoped not.

'I figure,' she said gently, 'that we both fight for control. I've been fighting for control for so long that it's going to be hard, but if...if you'd like us somehow to merge… If you could consider something like…joint control… If we could face Simon down together… And maybe…maybe if we could make a home for Harry to-gether?'

There was a gasp from Helen. Harry was staring, open-mouthed, trying to figure out what was going on. Even Maisie seemed stunned, but it didn't matter. All that mattered was the way Jack was looking at her.

'Kate…'

'Not if you don't want,' she said, hurriedly now, scared that she'd gone too far, read too much into what had hap-pened between them. 'I mean…in this new life…this new town you're going to…there'll be women there. You can get a housekeeper. Find someone else. Build a life. Move on.'

'So I could.' He sounded dazed.

'So, you see, you don't need me. It's just, if there's a position vacant…if I'd fit… You see, even if I don't run, I don't have to stay here. This is a place of healing. I be-lieve…somehow I seem to have healed. Somehow a doc-tor called Jack has worked his magic. But I don't depend on you, Jack. I can go anywhere. It's like the sea gates have been opened. I'm free.'

'So you are.'

'So you don't have to have me… I mean, if you do want to be alone…'

'Kate, shut up,' he said, sounding strained. 'Give me a moment to get things straight.'

So she shut up. She was having trouble getting things straight herself.

There was a long silence. Then… 'Harry?' Jack asked.

'Yep?' Harry seemed entranced. Puzzled but en-tranced.

'Your Aunt Helen hasn't met Hobble, or the rest of the team. How about you and Maisie go and introduce them?'

'I want to listen,' Helen said, and then she grinned and held up her hands as if in surrender. 'Fine,' she said. 'I have not the faintest clue what's going on, or maybe I do but I'm too gobsmacked to say anything. Harry, dolphins.'

'You want to give them some fish?'

'Yes,' Helen said. 'But, Jack...do you need anything before I go? For instance, I could lend you an engagement ring...'

'Helen...'

She threw up her hands again. 'Okay, just offering. Just loving this. I came over feeling sick. Now I feel...'

'Better?' Harry asked, anxious now. 'If you're sick, this place makes you better.'

'Well, you and Jack would know.' She grinned, a beatific grin that almost split her face. She took her nephew by the hand and she clicked her fingers for the dog. Where Helen ordered, dog would follow.

Maisie considered her, then dived into Harry's pile of belongings and grabbed a ball. And headed deliberately to the water.

'Uh-oh,' Kate said. 'Should we warn her?'

'Let's not,' Jack said, and tugged her closer. 'Kate.'

'Y-yes?' She was scared to breathe. How could she make so many assumptions? She'd thrown herself at him. Why? Because she was free?

It didn't matter if he didn't want her, she told herself—but she knew that it did.

It mattered so much...

'Kate, I'm trying to think this through,' he said. 'Bear with me if I falter. Let me think out loud.'

'Okay.' This was hopeful, she thought. Sort of.

'It seems to me,' he said, still holding her close, 'that somehow you seem to be taking control of your life. That's great. But in the next breath you're making an offer that takes my breath away. But I need to be honest. Kate, love, if you stay with me, there will be times that I try to be in control. I will get bossy. But, Kate, I'd like you to get bossy back. The way I see it, we'd be headed for something like flexible sea gates. Maybe we can go in and out together.'

'Oh, Jack…'

'But, Kate, this is fast.' He wasn't losing contact. The warmth and strength of him was flooding into her, making her feel…extraordinary. 'Love, even while I've been planning Harry's and my future, a future without you, more than I wanted anything in the world I've wanted you. That holds true now. But I won't hold you. I'm prepared to risk losing you if you want time to make up your mind. No strings attached. Just…loving each other until you decide…how free you want to be.'

'I don't want to be…that free,' she managed.

'But what about Harry? He's my responsibility. Not yours.'

'But if I want that responsibility? If I want the privilege of loving him?'

His hold on her tightened. She could feel his heartbeat under hers. She could feel the power of him. She could feel the love.

She held him back, and things were said in that moment with no words said. Vows were made in total silence.

Life shifted. The sea gates, locked for so long, creaked slowly open, and Jack was there, waiting for her to swim free with him.

'You'd want me?' he asked.

'More than anything in the world.'

'You'd leave here?'

'There are rehab. places for kids everywhere, and if

there aren't I can set them up. Someone else can take over my place here. Some other doctor who needs healing.'

'You no longer need healing?'

'I think,' she said unsteadily, 'that all I have is a void in my heart that needs filling. And I might...I just might be looking at a guy who could fill it.'

He smiled. He smiled and he smiled, and then he dropped to the sand.

On bended knee.

'I'm not sure if this is the time or the place,' he said. 'You need rose petals and champagne.'

'I don't need anything but you.'

She was smiling down at him. Smiling as much as he was. She was dizzy with smiling. Dizzy with...love?

This was all about Jack and the rest of her life.

'Then will you marry me?' Jack asked, and the world stilled.

She thought... Marriage. Jack. The feeling flooding through her... Who could describe it? Euphoria was too small a word.

'Is it too soon?' he said, mistaking her silence for hesitation. 'Kate, I can wait. I'll wait as long as I must. I'll do whatever I must to win you. To love you. But if you'll marry me I swear I'll not confine you. I swear I'll keep you free. All I'll do is love you, for as long as we both shall live.'

Silence. He needed her to answer, she thought desperately. She needed to get her voice in order, her thoughts in order. Somehow she made a massive effort.

'Jack, I've never had a family,' she said, softly and lovingly. 'Not really. I'm not sure how to start, but if you wouldn't mind taking on a raw beginner... You and me and Harry, and Maisie and whoever else comes along. Family. I'll do my best. I'll love you with all my heart and if that's not enough I'll love you some more. So, yes, Jack Kincaid, I'll marry you.'

She dropped to her knees to join him on the sand. He cupped her face in his hands, and looked at her, caressing her with his eyes.

'I will love you for ever,' he told her. 'I should have loved you and married you years ago but I'll make up for it. I have no idea how to be a husband, how to be a father, but I'll learn. The only requirement I know is love, and I have that in spades.'

'You, too?' She could barely speak. 'The way I feel...'

But she couldn't go on. He'd tilted her chin to kiss her. His mouth met hers. She felt his warmth, his strength and his love. His kiss was tender, loving, perfect, and it was the sealing of vows that were as yet unsaid but were already stronger than chains.

She kissed him back. His hand tugged her close and she surrendered to the kiss. She surrendered to this man but it was okay, it was fine, because he was surrendering, too.

She kissed him back. She loved him and held him and the kiss could have lasted forever, but finally, eventually, they became aware of laughter and applause around them.

They broke apart and patients, parents and staff were clustered around, smiling and smiling, ready to share in their joy.

Everyone but Helen.

Out on the sandbank Helen cut a lone figure, dripping wet, gesticulating hysterically as Maisie swam serenely back to shore.

Kate choked on laughter. She stood with Jack's arm around her while Maisie bounded up the beach to drop the ball at her feet.

'Oh, Maisie,' she faltered. 'How could you do that to Helen? Not when she's come all this way to warn me.'

'It'll be fine,' Jack said grandly, hugging her closer with one arm and waving to the beach in general with the other. 'Helen is family, and forgiveness come with the territory. I'm thinking family might take some getting used to, but we're about to start.' And he kissed her again. 'We might rescue Helen first, but we're about to start right now.'

Six months later... A coastal town south of Sydney. Sunday morning. They were down at the dolphin enclosure, watching Harry swim.

This was a different place from the dolphin sanctuary that had played such a huge part in their lives. This was simply an enclosure where injured dolphins were rehabilitated. Dolphins needing long-term care were sent somewhere like Dolphin Bay, but these were short-termers. They were wild dolphins, recovering from shark bites or encounters with fishing nets.

Jack and Kate had wed back at Dolphin Bay. It had seemed the only place. Helen had grumbled about needing to bring all her kids to the other side of the country but once her kids saw Dolphin Bay all grumbles were put aside.

The ceremony had been magic, on the beach at sunset. Kate had worn a simple dress, soft silk, floaty, beautiful. She'd worn frangipani in her hair, and nothing on her feet.

Harry and Maisie had been joint ring-bearers. Harry had carried the ring while Maisie had stood by his side, solemn and true, as if she'd understood the significance of the occasion. The fact that seagulls had intruded right after the ring ceremony and had needed to be chased was immaterial. Kate had been wed. A dog's duty was done.

Helen and Doug had beamed. The staff of Dolphin Bay had beamed as well. A new doctor had arrived the week before. Isabelle was a burnt-out surgeon. She'd arrived tentative, not sure if this could work, but after a week there was already colour in her cheeks, smiles, dolphin magic.

As for Simon, he was now nothing but a shadow from a forgotten past, safely back in prison for the foreseeable future.

Susie's father had done wonders, even finding outstanding charges that had nothing to do with Kate. 'And we'll have a watertight intervention order to protect you when he finally gets out,' Susie's dad had told them. 'Forget him.'

So they had. They'd moved on to happiness.

The staff of Dolphin Bay had given them a beach umbrella dotted with dolphins as a wedding gift. They were sitting under it now, while Harry lapped the pool. These dolphins in their new home weren't tame, but they seemed to lap with him.

'It's magic,' Kate whispered. 'We're so lucky.'

'Lucky indeed.' Jack held his wife's hand and thought of the last few months. The house they'd found, a beautiful cottage just back from the beach. His job, satisfying in a way he'd never dreamed. The new rehab centre Kate was setting up. Harry's school, where he was blossoming.

And this place...this dolphin sanctuary... They had such plans.

Because he'd spent his life so focussed on his career, Jack was financially secure. His money and Kate's skills had secured them seats on the board and already they had plans in place for expansion. Kate had visions of a bigger pool attached to a smaller hospital pool. She dreamed of an educational centre where kids could learn about the needs of wild dolphins.

She had hopes that one day kids might also come here to heal, just as they did at Dolphin Bay.

This was okay, Jack thought. Actually, this was more than okay. This was pretty much perfect.

'I don't want anything more in life than what I have right now,' he said, and he kissed his wife on the nose. And then, because who could resist, he kissed her on the lips.

She pushed him away, but just a little so she could still watch Harry. She was standing lifeguard, as all parents did. To Harry, the word 'Kate' was synonymous with 'Mum'. He loved Kate and she loved him right back. His parents would always be a part of his life, a loving memory, the foundations of his future, but he had his Jack and his Kate and he was as happy as a kid could be.

Actually, he had an extra lifeguard as well. Maisie was standing guard on the sidelines. She wasn't allowed in the dolphin pool but everyone knew that one hint of trouble she'd be in there. Harry was hers.

'So you don't want anything else?' Kate asked, as they watched, and Jack thought about it.

'A beer,' he conceded. 'In a while. But that's pretty much it.'

'That's a shame,' she told him. 'Because I have something for you.'

'What?'

And in answer she took his hand. She was wearing a bikini. Her stomach was smooth and flat, yet when she held his hand over it and pressed down he felt…he felt…

'You really want nothing else?' she asked.

He closed his eyes, and when he opened them he'd come to a decision.

'Harry,' he called. 'Time to come out.'

'Aw…'

'No arguments,' he called. 'Out, now.'

So Harry reluctantly emerged. Maisie met him, boy

and dog hugged—they'd been separated for a whole fifteen minutes!—and then he turned to Jack.

'Why did I have to get out?' he demanded.

'Because lifesaving duties have been suspended,' Jack
told him. 'Harry, could you pour yourself a drink and go
sit in the shade with Maisie?'

'Why?'

'Because there's something I need to do,' he told him.
'Our Kate has just given me a gift, something so priceless
I can scarcely take it in. I love you, mate, but right now I
need to devote all my time to telling Kate I love her. So
you concentrate on your soda and your dog while I take
our Kate into my arms and tell her I love her for ever.'

'Can I help?' Harry asked.

'Join the queue,' Jack said. 'But don't rush. Loving
Kate's important, and we have all the time in the world.'

* * * * *

Mills & Boon® Hardback
September 2014

ROMANCE

The Housekeeper's Awakening	Sharon Kendrick
More Precious than a Crown	Carol Marinelli
Captured by the Sheikh	Kate Hewitt
A Night in the Prince's Bed	Chantelle Shaw
Damaso Claims His Heir	Annie West
Changing Constantinou's Game	Jennifer Hayward
The Ultimate Revenge	Victoria Parker
Tycoon's Temptation	Trish Morey
The Party Dare	Anne Oliver
Sleeping with the Soldier	Charlotte Phillips
All's Fair in Lust & War	Amber Page
Dressed to Thrill	Bella Frances
Interview with a Tycoon	Cara Colter
Her Boss by Arrangement	Teresa Carpenter
In Her Rival's Arms	Alison Roberts
Frozen Heart, Melting Kiss	Ellie Darkins
After One Forbidden Night...	Amber McKenzie
Dr Perfect on Her Doorstep	Lucy Clark

MEDICAL

A Secret Shared...	Marion Lennox
Flirting with the Doc of Her Dreams	Janice Lynn
The Doctor Who Made Her Love Again	Susan Carlisle
The Maverick Who Ruled Her Heart	Susan Carlisle

0814GEN STD HB

Mills & Boon® Large Print
September 2014

ROMANCE

The Only Woman to Defy Him	Carol Marinelli
Secrets of a Ruthless Tycoon	Cathy Williams
Gambling with the Crown	Lynn Raye Harris
The Forbidden Touch of Sanguardo	Julia James
One Night to Risk it All	Maisey Yates
A Clash with Cannavaro	Elizabeth Power
The Truth About De Campo	Jennifer Hayward
Expecting the Prince's Baby	Rebecca Winters
The Millionaire's Homecoming	Cara Colter
The Heir of the Castle	Scarlet Wilson
Twelve Hours of Temptation	Shoma Narayanan

HISTORICAL

Unwed and Unrepentant	Marguerite Kaye
Return of the Prodigal Gilvry	Ann Lethbridge
A Traitor's Touch	Helen Dickson
Yield to the Highlander	Terri Brisbin
Return of the Viking Warrior	Michelle Styles

MEDICAL

Waves of Temptation	Marion Lennox
Risk of a Lifetime	Caroline Anderson
To Play with Fire	Tina Beckett
The Dangers of Dating Dr Carvalho	Tina Beckett
Uncovering Her Secrets	Amalie Berlin
Unlocking the Doctor's Heart	Susanne Hampton

Mills & Boon® Hardback
October 2014

ROMANCE

An Heiress for His Empire	Lucy Monroe
His for a Price	Caitlin Crews
Commanded by the Sheikh	Kate Hewitt
The Valquez Bride	Melanie Milburne
The Uncompromising Italian	Cathy Williams
Prince Hafiz's Only Vice	Susanna Carr
A Deal Before the Altar	Rachael Thomas
Rival's Challenge	Abby Green
The Party Starts at Midnight	Lucy King
Your Bed or Mine?	Joss Wood
Turning the Good Girl Bad	Avril Tremayne
Breaking the Bro Code	Stefanie London
The Billionaire in Disguise	Soraya Lane
The Unexpected Honeymoon	Barbara Wallace
A Princess by Christmas	Jennifer Faye
His Reluctant Cinderella	Jessica Gilmore
One More Night with Her Desert Prince...	Jennifer Taylor
From Fling to Forever	Avril Tremayne

MEDICAL

It Started with No Strings...	Kate Hardy
Flirting with Dr Off-Limits	Robin Gianna
Dare She Date Again?	Amy Ruttan
The Surgeon's Christmas Wish	Annie O'Neil

Mills & Boon® Large Print

October 2014

ROMANCE

HISTORICAL

MEDICAL

MILLS & BOON®

Why shop at millsandboon.co.uk?

Each year, thousands of romance readers find their perfect read at millsandboon.co.uk. That's because we're passionate about bringing you the very best romantic fiction. Here are some of the advantages of shopping at www.millsandboon.co.uk:

* **Get new books first**—you'll be able to buy your favourite books one month before they hit the shops

* **Get exclusive discounts**—you'll also be able to buy our specially created monthly collections, with up to 50% off the RRP

* **Find your favourite authors**—latest news, interviews and new releases for all your favourite authors and series on our website, plus ideas for what to try next

* **Join in**—once you've bought your favourite books, don't forget to register with us to rate, review and join in the discussions

Visit **www.millsandboon.co.uk**
for all this and more today!